BLOOD MONEY

Charlie Rutland specialized in scandal-hunting. As a journalist on a smart magazine, his job was to search out anything that could be turned into a good smear story. Then, while carrying out some 'investigations' in Yorkshire, his career came to an abrupt and violent end. Inspector Crow, skeletal as ever, arrives from Scotland Yard to find a formidable task awaiting him. He uncovers some strange facts connected with Rutland's death – a Nazi war criminal, an old vagrant of the dales, and in a dead man's diary the number of a stolen car belonging to an attractive and wealthy widow.

BLOOD MONEY

BLOOD MONEY

by

Roy Lewis

Magna Large Print Books
Long Preston, North Yorkshire,
BD23 4ND, England.

British Library Cataloguing in Publication Data.

Lewis, Roy
    Blood money.

    A catalogue record of this book is
    available from the British Library

    ISBN   978-0-7505-4130-5

First published in Great Britain by
Templar North Publishing Ltd.

Copyright © Roy Lewis 1973 and 2012

Cover illustration © Benjamin Harte by arrangement with
Arcangel Images

The author asserts the moral right to be identified as the author
of this work

Published in Large Print 2015 by arrangement with
Roy Lewis

Magna Large Print is an imprint of Library Magna Books Ltd.

Printed and bound in Great Britain by
T.J. (International) Ltd., Cornwall, PL28 8RW

Chapter 1

1

The crowd in the public bar was usual for a Friday night. Charlie Rutland finished his drink, wiped a hand across his mouth and made his way out of the bar.

He walked into the narrow passageway and the handle of the door marked PRIVATE squealed as he turned it. The room beyond was cold and dark, and Rutland's nose wrinkled in distaste as he caught the odours of stale food from the kitchen beyond. He hurried through to the stairway and climbed quickly to the floor above. His step was soft as he walked along the landing. Too heavy a tread made the lights above the bar shiver and Bert would be down there.

He opened the door of the spare room, crossed its cold darkness to the electric fire and depressed a switch. The bars glowed, emitting a strengthening heat, and Charlie sat on the edge of the bed.

He stared at the fire and chuckled. Whisky

warmed his veins and exultation still bubbled in his blood. He sat and waited and the minutes slipped past: he had time on his hands and nothing better to do until the early hours of the morning. He waited for Doris and soon she came.

She entered the room, closed the door behind her and stood staring at him in the dimness. He could smell the sourness of her perfume, defeated by hours behind the bar, and it made him feel irritated, and yet excited too. He moved freely in Europe and he had met many women, but not this kind. She was easy, she was earthy, she was big – and Charlie Rutland normally went for the small, controlled, sophisticated woman who could be bought by dinner or a drink.

Doris was different. She gave enthusiastically, and without control. She disgusted him in a way, and he expressed his disgust by leaving money for her, each time. Yet he was back here again, tonight. Previously it had arisen out of boredom and preoccupation with other important matters. She provided him with release from sexual tensions with no cloying pretences demanded. Tonight ... it was different. It would be the last time, for his period in Yorkshire was almost over.

'You went too far tonight, Charlie.'

Her tone was reproving as she stepped forward, shaking her blonde head. When he said nothing she went on. 'I don't mind a joke, but some of the cracks you made down there, they could make Bert suspicious–'

'Bert knows,' Charlie said flatly.

'He doesn't exactly *know*–'

Charlie Rutland looked up at Doris and sneered. She was a heavily built woman, as tall as he was. She possessed none of the qualities he normally sought in a woman, but somehow she had been fitting to these weeks, grovelling around, digging, searching among the dingy towns and the dales of Yorkshire.

'Of course he knows. I leave the bar, you leave the bar. He'd be blind if he didn't notice after these weeks. And where does he think the money comes from, for God's sake? I don't know what sort of arrangement you two have between you, but don't try to tell me he doesn't know that I've been laying you.'

'Charlie, that's enough!' Doris looked large and menacing in the faint light. 'All right, so he ... guesses, but what we got between us is nothing to do with it. Guessing ... and knowin', they're different, and some of the remarks you made tonight was shovin' it down his throat.'

Charlie laughed, rose and stood grinning at her silently. She shook her head. 'I don't know what's got into you tonight, Charlie. You're wound up tight, seems to me–'

'It's victory,' he said, and reached for her. 'And how better to celebrate the brink of victory than to sleep with a big, easy whore–'

Doris swung at him quickly but he shoved her from him.

Doris staggered back on her high heels, teetered crazily until she fetched up against the wall with a breathless thump. Her mouth fell open and her heel struck the electric fire: it sparkled crazily, crackled, and then, after a moment's stupefied silence, Doris squealed low and came forward, lunging. She missed completely with her right hand, but her left took Charlie across the cheekbone. He staggered back, raised his arms as Doris swung two-handed at his head, raging, cuffing him, pounding at him. The breath whistled from her mouth, her splendid breasts rose and fell, and the rhythm of her attack slowed, grew less regular as her wind and inclination lessened.

Charlie was laughing. His arms were up, his hands protecting his face and he was laughing uncontrollably. Doris realized he was almost hysterical. Her attack had only caused him amusement, and yet what he was saying over and over seemed to bear no relation to her, or her reaction. She stopped suddenly, and turned away, in anger and resentment.

Charlie stopped laughing immediately. He reached for her, grabbed her, and though she struggled for a moment it was a token only, for though resentment forced her to show unwillingness, this was not the first time for them and she knew his hands and his body.

Soon, in the darkness, she was knowing them again. And yet it was not like other times, it was different.

Charlie was more violent, uncontrolled, and she felt as though all the pent-up fires of a long abstinence were blazing at her. He was shuddering, but there was a maniac laughter still bubbling in his chest and she felt a stranger to him. He had always enjoyed the animal, mother warmth of her body, the size and spread of her limbs, and his small frame had clung to hers on occasions ... but not tonight. This time he used her, hard, cruel, unpleasant. She knew there never had been affection: this was little more than business and pleasure mixed. Tonight, she sensed the viciousness of a man tasting a new success.

When he cooled in sexual exhaustion she lay still, unsatisfied, a little afraid. When he left the bed and dressed he said nothing. He left the money as usual, on the dressing table near the window. And when he had gone she felt cold, and miserable and angry.

This had been bad.

Bert came up at 2 a.m.

He put on the bedside light, bending over her to do it, and wide-awake still, she smelt the fetid, beery breath. Through half-lidded eyes she watched him remove his shirt and vest: thickly muscled shoulders ran down to a heavy waist. Bert grinned at himself, admiring his body. 'Not bad, hey, Doris? In spite of the beer it's still all there, isn't it? More than you can say for some of them pansies in the bar.'

He finished undressing. His legs were thin, heavily veined.

'Boxers' legs,' he said admiringly. He stood upright, six inches taller than Charlie, heavy, muscled, tough. 'Look out, woman, I'm comin' for yer.'

Petulantly, Doris shrugged deeper under the bedclothes.

'Not tonight, Bert, for God's sake. And cover yourself up, you look ridiculous.'

It was a mistake, she knew it as soon as she said it, but it had come out because of Charlie and his attitude tonight, and his contempt and the way he had used her. When Bert replied his voice was steady, but there was a cold edge to it. 'What the hell do you mean?'

'I'm sorry, Bert, I didn't mean that, it's just with the bar and everything I'm tired. Let's give it a miss tonight.'

'What happened?'

Doris was in no mood for questions. 'What the hell do you think happened? Nothing. The money's over there, so why don't you just come to bed and go to sleep? Do you have to prove yourself all the time?'

Bert clenched his fists. 'I don't have to prove nothing. I'm twice that pansy's age and twice the man too. He never could satisfy you, you know that, not the way I do.'

The silence was ugly. Doris lay stiff in the bed, suddenly frightened.

'Come to bed, Bert,' she whispered.

He stood still, naked, ludicrous, furious. 'You been lying to me?'

The shadows of resentment left by Charlie Rutland suddenly took form and substance, and almost without thinking Doris leaned up in bed and screamed at Bert.

'Lying, hell! Get to bed and stop prancing like a stud racehorse! I'm sick of your thundering at me every time he's been here. It's the only time you want to do it – what's the matter, you need Charlie Rutland to get you working? Can't you grind yourself up to it unless you know he's been with me first? What happens down in the bar – do you picture him up here, and does that make you want me, afterwards? Prove yourself, to *me?* You've nothing to prove – you never were any damned good and you've got worse as you've got older! You always had the inclination but the flesh was never strong, was it?'

Bert swore at her. He swore loudly and profanely.

Then he advanced towards the bed. 'I'll damn well show you,' he said.

2

When the perspiration had turned to ice along his back he shivered. He lay quiet for a while; Doris's reluctant body still lay, unmoving, under his. There was contempt in her stiffness. He felt beaten, humiliated.

14

He could not hide the querulousness in his tone. 'You always said he was no good. You always said I was better, I was the best. You always said–'

His voice trailed away, gone like his strength. He had known about Charlie, they had laughed at his open interest in Doris, and Bert had not objected too much to Charlie Rutland coming up here. Doris was a woman who needed men, he knew that, but he had always thought … she had always said…

Her heavy body stirred angrily.

'All right, you big oaf. You can get off now. You're not going to make it, so call it a night.'

He lurched away from her, rolled to the edge of the bed. The night air seared his heated chest with a cold edge. The strength had drained from him in his desperation but that had been a sexual strength; now, hate was building up a knot of power inside him that demanded expression. Slowly he climbed from her and sat on the edge of the bed, his head lowered like a spent bull.

'Now you know, don't you,' Doris said spitefully. Bert ignored her. He stood up, breathed deeply, expanded his broad chest. He reached for his clothes. She watched him dress.

'Where the hell are you going?' she asked.

Bert made no reply. He finished dressing and headed for the door. Doris sat up in bed and screamed at him. 'I asked you a question!'

Bert turned to look at her. His face was stiff and he found difficulty in getting out the words.

'I'll kill him,' he said. 'I will. I'll kill the bastard.'

It was about three in the morning. Sleep was still far from Charlie Rutland. He sat in the chair and the glass of brandy glowed in his hand. It tasted like triumph in his mouth and he liked the taste, he savoured it, for just when disaster had seemed to overtake him and all the planning had been for nothing, he'd found the jackpot again, the end of the rainbow.

Time had moved slowly tonight. He had gone to the Three Bells, taken a few drinks, caught Doris's glance and thought – why not, it'll pass the time. A big easy whore, one he needn't court or think about when he had other, more serious matters on his mind. But they were resolved now, and he'd told Doris, shown her what he really thought of her tonight. She'd served a purpose. Now he was leaving Yorkshire he could return to the kind of women that really interested him. Doris ... an experience, big, spreading, but ultimately distasteful.

Soon, in the morning, he'd be going south. Ideas and plans began to tumble over themselves in his head like eager puppies. He finished his brandy, rose to pour another, and the doorbell buzzed, then buzzed again.

Charlie Rutland paused, then with a confident air he walked towards the front door of the bungalow. He fumbled with the catch, and briefly he wondered just how much money there would be, in the end. Then he flung open the door, his lips framing a greeting.

He caught one quick glimpse of the dark shape before his nose cracked and splintered and the blood gushed over his flowered shirt. He fell backwards and something heavy struck his ribs, sending the breath rushing out of his lungs. He tried to scream in pain and fear but there was only silence.

And then the silence was without end.

Chapter 2

1

There was a Pakistani ticket collector on duty at the barrier on Leeds railway station when Detective Chief Inspector John Crow left the train. He flickered an interested glance at Crow as he passed through the barrier. Crow wore no hat and his domed skull drew the man's attention; his deep-set eyes and curved, jutting nose held the man's curiosity; and Crow had no doubt that as he walked away across the echoing hallway his height and general scrawniness would retain the man's interest until he had vanished from sight.

'There's one thing, John,' Martha sometimes said, 'people don't forget you easily.'

She meant he was often remembered for his kindness to old folk in the area where they lived, and for the quiet warmth of his personality, but he was not blind to the effect his physical appearance could have on those he faced for the first time.

The ticket collector would remember him all right. Detective-Inspector Wilson was standing beside the car in the forecourt. A uniformed constable hovered uneasily nearby, one eye on the limited waiting sign. As Crow came across, Wilson gave him a tight little smile and nodded. They hadn't seen each other for three months: they'd been on different cases, miles apart. The demands of the Murder Squad could do that.

'They didn't tell me you were assigned to this investigation,' Crow said.

'I arrived this morning, sir. I was on leave in Harrogate – so I was on hand. I've fixed us up with rooms at a hotel at Backchapel – I know the owner and he can offer us all the facilities we need. It's only seven miles from the scene of crime too, and I thought you'd prefer HQ there, rather than in town,'

He opened the car door and took Crow's luggage from him, placed it in the boot and slid behind the wheel.

With a wave to the now happier constable, he turned the car and headed for City Square. Over his shoulder he said, 'Dinner's at eight. The scene of crime unit has been out at the murdered man's bungalow all day, forensic have been there too, the liaison officer will be calling to pick us up in the morning – his name's Jones – I've been in touch with the Yard for a dossier and I've cleared things with the Chief Constable. So–'

'So there's no need for me to turn out until morning?'

Wilson ducked his head slightly and pulled the car into the traffic heading for Huddersfield. 'I thought I could let you have all the details I've gleaned so far over dinner this evening. I've got some papers–'

'You've had a busy day,' Crow said.

Wilson changed lanes, pulled ahead of a sedate Morris, changed lanes again. He knew the road well.

'It's a home patch,' he said. 'I spent eight years in the Bradford force before I joined the Mets, and there are still a few people I know. Moreover, a Bradford accent can work wonders among the lads. Makes them realize even Murder Squad people are still folk.'

Crow smiled. He had worked with Wilson for several years. He knew him for a taciturn, dependable man, relatively short of speech and enthusiasm, occasionally right-wing in his attitudes, rarely excited, never ebullient.

Being in Leeds and working in Yorkshire seemed to be bringing him as near to ebullience as he could possibly be. And it was obviously having its effect upon his work rate.

They left Leeds and crossed the motorway, then swung left into a long hill-road that looped above huddled grey stone houses shouldering their way down the slopes in long terraces. The late sun dipped over the hill before they reached the top, and the distant moors had a purple tinge in the fading light. A long bank of cloud caught the dying rays and transmuted them into wisps of gold.

The white-painted, decaying sign said Backchapel.

From the window of his room Crow could see a stream tumbling whitely in the gathering darkness, falling to the iron bridge that led down to the town. The hotel stood perched at the north end of Backchapel: its spacious car park told of its popularity as a pub, its select room decked in red and blue and gold showed it catered for the expensive gin and whisky trade, and the muted sounds of the juke box in the back room illustrated the proprietor's wisdom in segregating the young from the regular.

The dining-room was small, the table-cloths were white and clean, the menu was simple but good. Crow decided it would do. He told Wilson so, over coffee.

'I thought it would,' Wilson said. 'Joe Bembridge is an old friend and he runs a good hostelry. And he'll leave us well alone. There's three rooms top of the landing we can use as an HQ when we're not wanting the station facilities. I've got the papers up there.'

Crow sipped his coffee, held the cup between long, predatory fingers.

'You can let me have the details now. I'll see the papers later.'

Wilson nodded, pushed his chair back from the table and folded his arms. His broad face was slightly flushed: Crow had seen red wine do that for him before. It did not affect his mental capacities.

'The dead man was called Charles Rutland. Thirty-six years old, five feet eight inches, slimly built, about ten stone in weight, dark curly hair, blue eyes.'

'Sounds like a passport description.'

'Some of it is. We found his passport in his wallet inside a travelling case. He's done a bit of globe-trotting: most recently, West Germany.'

'In what capacity?'

Wilson frowned slightly. 'I wondered whether you might have heard of him. He writes for *Scathe* magazine.'

For a moment Crow had thought the

frown was for his lack of perspicacity in not knowing the name Rutland; now he realized Wilson was simply showing his customary displeasure at anything concerned with leftwing activity, radicalism, pornography or overt sex.

'*Scathe* magazine,' Crow murmured.

'You'll know the magazine, sir,' Wilson said stiffly. 'Rubbish.'

Crow knew it all right. It had arisen during the satirical boom in the fifties, but it had pursued a different course than its contemporaries. It had not sought to lampoon; rather, it had set out to make as much money out of sensationalism as it possibly could. In general, it had steered clear of important people who could have hurt it – at least, unless it was pretty certain of its facts. There had been three lawsuits in its first five years, and several near misses. Two police investigations had been mounted but they had been abortive: *Scathe* sailed close to the wind but employed excellent company lawyers and existed this side of libel. Of recent years it had started to take itself a little more seriously – aiming shafts at political figures, but even so the mixture was largely as before: political dirt, sexual titillation, veiled insult, the knowing finger along the nose.

As Wilson had said – rubbish, but nasty too.

'I've carried out checks with the local police and they tell me Rutland rented a bungalow at Earston a month or so back. It looks as though he felt like escaping from London from time to time.'

'Odd,' Crow said. 'I mean, a man who travels around a great deal, renting a place in Yorkshire. You'd have thought he'd have settled for something more exotic.'

'I wouldn't, sir,' Wilson said, and looked Crow in the eye. Crow smiled.

'All right. Go on.'

'As far as I can make out, Rutland came up here, looked around for a suitable place, rented the bungalow and then moved in. He must have been taking some leave, for he spent quite a bit of time around here. He had no car but he hired one to take him around – I've not been able to speak to the driver because he's off on a fishing holiday in the Lake District and no one seems to know where he went, exactly. He's expected back end of the week. One thing seems fairly clear – Rutland certainly took in some countryside in his hired car.'

Crow finished his coffee and pushed the cup away. 'Tell me about the killing.'

'Rutland was lying in the hall of the bung-alow. As far as I can make out he'd answered the door and been attacked immediately. His face is badly marked, nose broken and so on, but he was killed by the blows struck to the top of his head. Forensic have a bloodstained poker – it looks like the murder weapon.'

'Did Rutland put up much of a struggle?'

'Don't think so.' Wilson hesitated doubt-fully. 'Maybe it happened too quickly for him to defend himself – he couldn't even have raised his hands. He must have been knocked backwards before he could do a thing. There's not much by way of signs of a struggle in that hall.'

'We'll take a look in the morning,' Crow said. 'Right now I'll have a look at the notes you've produced, and then it'll be an early night. It could be the last one we'll have for a while.'

2

The bungalow was unassuming, grey stone, crouched at the far end of Earston village and shadowed by the looming hill beyond. The village itself was little more than a huddle of terraced cottages, once used by the mill workers down at the bottom of the hill. The chimneys were quiet now, the mill derelict, and the cottages had not yet been caught up by the desire for country residences by the middle-class members of the town areas. Crow doubted whether they would be – except for Charles Rutland. The valley looked bleak and desolate to him. He felt a stranger here.

The police constable on duty in the weed-ridden front garden saluted him as he made his way towards the door. Inside the bungalow, Wilson introduced him to Detective-Sergeant Jones, the liaison officer. He was a sallow, dark-haired man who was unduly polite, almost to the edge of servility. Perhaps this was the first time he'd worked with Murder Squad people.

The man who came out of the sitting-room was introduced as Dr Frust. He was small, dapper in a check shirt and bright bow-tie, and his eyes twinkled behind pince-nez glasses. There was something irrepressibly cheerful in his manner: Crow had seen it before among Home Office pathologists. He suspected it was a defence mechanism against horror.

'I've just been carrying out some further checks in the sitting-room,' Frust said. 'And

I had a look around the fireplace. I'd wondered about it, you see. The killer would hardly have wanted to be seen walking the streets with a poker, would he? Come here.'

He beckoned, and Crow followed him into the sitting-room. It was about fifteen feet long, with an old sash window at the far end. The fireplace to which Frust pointed was as old as the window: the whole place needed considerable modernization. Crow couldn't imagine why Rutland would have wanted to rent it. Frust was standing near the dead coal fire.

'You see? There's a stand here – no poker, just a dustpan and brush. But that's where the poker came from. And Rutland was murdered in the hall.'

'No sign of a struggle in here?' Crow asked sharply. Frust and Wilson answered together, in the negative, and Frust chuckled.

'Deduction's not strictly my business, I just deal in facts, but I never could resist hypotheses. If you want my view, this is how it went: Rutland was sitting there – see his glass, placed on the table? He was having a drink – brandy – when the bell went. He put down the drink, walked out, opened the front door and – *wham!*'

Frust readjusted his glasses and grinned.

'I've had a quick look at the body and Rutland took quite a beating around the face. A few kicks in the ribs too, I suspect – I think there may be fractures of the rib cage. But after all this when Rutland was lying there in the hallway, the killer took second wind, came in here, looked around for a suitable weapon, picked up the poker and beat Rutland's head in. Just like that.'

'Messy,' Crow said grimly.

'Very. But deliberate.'

'You can't say exactly when all this took place?'

Frust blinked. 'Oh, give us time, Chief Inspector. It's too early yet. We took some rectal readings but they're hardly accurate–'

'Give me a rough estimate.'

'It'll be very rough,' Frust said, frowning. 'But I'd say all this happened pretty late at night – maybe even during the early hours of the morning.'

'A late caller,' Crow said. 'Anything else you can give us so far?'

Frust grinned delightedly. 'There's a general routine about these investigations, as you know, and it'll take us some little time to sort out time of death, cause of death and so on. But I've got one assistant down at the lab who's rather kinky about one aspect of all cadavers. He enjoys his work, so I let him indulge himself immediately Rutland came in on the blood wagon.'

'So?'

Frust's grin widened. 'He tells me Charles Rutland probably had sexual intercourse not too long before he died.'

'How long?' Crow asked sharply.

Frust spread his hands wide.

'Can't tell that, until we work out the time of death. But I'll be in touch. Nice to meet you.'

Wilson's mouth was rather stiff. Crow took the official photographs of the dead man from his briefcase and studied them in relation to the dark marks on the hall carpet.

'Sex ... and *Scathe* magazine. That'll do to start with.'

'Sir?'

Crow put the photograph back in the briefcase and looked at Wilson. 'Personal life and business life, the old story, Wilson. In this case, you take one, I'll take the other. You're the local man, you talk the lingo. I want you to go through this bungalow with a fine toothcomb, get anything you can on Charles Rutland. And I want you to conduct the local enquiries: I want to know what Rutland's been up to here on his vacation, if that's what it was. I want to know where he's been going and who he's been going with. It may be you'll be able to turn up some local gossip about a woman he's been seeing. If he has had sexual intercourse recently I want you to find his partner. We'll have questions to ask of her.'

'Yes, sir. And I think I'd better talk to the owner of the bungalow too. He's a local man, lives in Batley. He may be able to throw some light on Rutland's activities.'

Crow nodded, satisfied. 'Good. I'll want to have a good look around here and then I'm going along to see the Chief Constable, make sure everything's smooth on the liaison front. I'll also want to put out a statement to the Press before they start hounding us. I'll be at the hotel this evening and we can have another talk after dinner, but then I'll be leaving you to get on with investigating Rutland's movements in Yorkshire.'

He walked away towards the bedroom. Over his shoulder he said, 'I'll be off to London in the morning. I want to have a talk with *Scathe* magazine.'

Chapter 3

1

Earl Robson set great store by appearance.

He sat in his office at *Scathe* magazine dressed in his grey suit, grey suede shoes, grey silk shirt and grey-pink tie but he knew he was not a grey person: his handsome tan, black hair and white teeth backed up a confidence of manner that told the world he was a success at forty and liked it. He used his face and his slim figure the way an actor would, always conscious of angles, always aware of an audience, always controlled in his attitudes. He had piercing blue eyes and heavy eyebrows: he could bring thunderclouds to his features with the latter, lightning with the former.

At this moment his eyebrows were faintly surprised, his eyes sardonic, as he observed the man seated in front of him.

Tall, over six feet; hairless skull and bushy eyebrows; an expensive suit whose cut could not conceal the awkward gangling nature of the body that inhabited it; thin bony wrists and long fingers like talons.

Decidedly unprepossessing, and therefore not a man of account.

'I suppose,' he said coolly, 'you've come on account of Charlie Rutland.'

Detective Chief Inspector Crow's eyes were calm.

He nodded slowly. 'That's right. You've heard about it then?'

Robson managed a sneer without detracting overmuch from his good looks. 'It was in the newspapers yesterday. Battered to death, I understand.'

'You don't seem unduly concerned about it.'

'My dear man,' Robson drawled as he picked up a gold-topped pencil from the broad desk and began to play with it, 'is there any reason why I should be over-concerned?'

'Rutland was an employee of yours.'

'And a good one. Oh, I'll admit that quite freely. Charlie Rutland was one of our best men – but that isn't to say we haven't got others, and there are plenty of men only too eager to step into his shoes. You see, Inspector, *Scathe* magazine is a profitable journal, it pays high fees and demands good copy. We can replace Rutland easily enough.'

34

'You surprise me. I thought good journalists were difficult to find,' Crow said mildly.

'Ah, but in our kind of journalism–' Robson stopped suddenly. He was vaguely aware that he had been caught in a corner and he didn't like it. He showed no sign of being ruffled, however. 'Let's just say we can replace him. Now then ... I'm not at all sure that I'll be able to help you in your enquiries into his death.'

'There are a number of questions I'd like to ask you, nevertheless. First of all, I understand Rutland was on leave – did he often spend his leave in Yorkshire?'

Robson tossed the pencil languidly upon the desk and watched it roll. 'Leave? I don't know where you got that idea.'

'You mean he was working up there?'

'I imagine so, yes.'

Crow raised his bushy eyebrows. His voice was very quiet. Robson had noticed this with many men who came into his office: he had a presence, an appearance of aristocratic ennui that unsettled people. He cultivated it. It would account for this policeman's quietness.

'You *imagine* so, Mr Robson?'

'Well, let me put it like this. Rutland was a good man. He's been on the magazine for

35·

some years. I could tru – I knew he'd bring up the goods if given his head. So, when he went off to the wilds of Yorkshire that was all right by me. He was working on a story–'

'What story?'

Robson did not care for interruptions. He raised an eyebrow and sniffed. 'You should know better than that, Inspector. Journalists don't discuss stories or sources.'

'No? They sometimes get sent to prison if they won't.' Crow said with the hint of a smile. Robson decided the smile denoted nervousness. He made no reply and after a moment Crow said, 'Tell me about Rutland.'

Robson shrugged indifferently. 'I told you, he was a good journalist. He came up with very printable material. He had a nose for a...' He almost said 'scandal'. He changed it smoothly. 'For a good story.'

'Could you let me see some of his stories of recent months?'

'Our library is at your disposal.'

'I suppose these stories he wrote, they could make him enemies?'

Earl Robson exposed his teeth in a warm smile at the underestimation the policeman displayed. The warmth of his smile found no reflection in his eyes. 'Enemies! My dear man, to put it in the vernacular, he had more

36

enemies than we've had hot dinners. Let me say this about Charlie Rutland: he made enemies with the good copy he produced, but he made almost as many enemies among the people he met. Charlie Rutland,' he added feelingly, 'was a right bastard.'

'In what way?'

'You name it.'

Crow shrugged and contemplated his hands. 'Perhaps you could give me some names?'

Robson swung his chair from side to side in an easy, soothing motion. He smiled again, half closed his eyes and ticked off the names on his fingers. 'Edwards, Holmes, Dick Shaw, Phil Peters, Dawnay, Acton and Squires, Sims – will they do for a start?'

Crow was staring at him impassively. For a moment, Robson wondered whether he had summed up the man wrongly, but Robson was not accustomed to making such admissions to himself.

'You're on a very long trail, Inspector, believe me.'

'It may be that I could find a few short cuts,' Crow replied. His tone remained quiet as he added, 'For instance, the name Earl Robson was not among those you mentioned.'

Robson's chair stopped swinging. He glared at the skeletal figure of the policeman sitting upright in the chair facing him. Could the man have already made enquiries? Could he already know about Rutland and Sandra?

'I don't think I cared for that remark,' he said, letting the steel slip into his voice. Crow was, surprisingly, unmoved.

'And I don't care about your feelings, Mr Robson. I'm here to ask questions. You said Rutland made enemies easily, and you spoke with feeling. Were you one of his enemies?'

'I was his employer.'

'That's no answer to the question.'

'I...' Robson began to move his chair again but the smooth rhythm had gone. He watched the policeman, and thought back over the months. He had been divorced almost a year ago; Sandra had returned three months ago; there was no official connection between Rutland and Sandra, so Crow could know nothing. He shook his head, positively and confidently.

'I was Rutland's employer. I will be completely frank and say I didn't like him, but I didn't have to – it was his copy I was interested in. As managing editor and proprietor of *Scathe* I could afford to ignore his insolence, crudity, ill manners and bad taste, just as long as he brought in his stories. Equally, I can afford to ignore his death. It doesn't touch me.'

'A death can touch us all, Mr Robson.' Crow leaned forward, linked his long fingers, right hand to left. 'Let's get back to the Yorkshire story.'

'I told you, I–'

'No, you *didn't* tell me. So I'm asking again.' Surprise touched Robson. He tried to smile but was conscious of its stiffness. This man touched him with ice, and few had been able to do that.

'I ... I can't have made myself clear. Rutland was a law unto himself. He went to Yorkshire, told me he was on a story. I don't know what it was. It certainly might have been about something that could have led to his death, but I don't know.'

'What story was he working on previously?'

'I really can't go ahead and–'

'*Robson.*' Crow's voice had changed; the mildness had faded, it was still quiet but it held hints of menace. 'I'm beginning to feel you're wasting my time. I haven't time to waste. This is a murder investigation. Give me your assistance. If you don't, I'll do more than demand it. I'll take it.'

It was an empty threat, it was no threat, there was nothing a policeman could do to Earl Robson, but Robson felt the blood draining from under his tan, felt it physically like a weakening of strength.

'I'm telling you the truth. I know nothing about the Yorkshire thing. His previous story … it wasn't finished.'

'The German story?'

Robson's eyes widened as he stared at Crow in surprise. 'How do you know?'

'His passport.'

Robson was annoyed with himself as he caught the contempt in Crow's tone.

'He's recently come back from West Germany. I presume he was chasing up some story. What was it?' Earl Robson hesitated. This was a line he didn't want followed: an early investigation by Crow could well damage the chances of the Berlin story.

'He went to a trade fair in Berlin.' The words came out in spite of himself. 'He picked up a story while he was there and stayed on to follow it up.'

'And?'

'Nothing. That's all there is to it. He came back, told me the story wasn't on. So we killed it. Then a few days later he went off to Yorkshire.'

'What was the story in Berlin?'

Robson waved his hands helplessly. 'It was killed, I tell you. There's no point–'

'Robson, I'll decide whether it has point or not. I want to know. Who was involved?'

His bushy eyebrows were frowning; his thin lips set firmly. Robson reached for a cigarette out of the gold-topped box that matched the pencil, and lit the cigarette with a gold lighter. His hand did not shake.

'I can't tell you very much about it. Over the phone Rutland said he had a story about a German businessman that needed following up. I gave him the go ahead, expenses and so on. But it all died when–'

'*Names*, Mr Robson.'

Unhappily, Robson said, 'Gunther. Conrad Gunther. I don't know that–'

'Tell me about him. Mr Robson.'

2

'I tell you, I don't know that there's a great deal I can produce for you. We did some checking of our own, of course – as soon as Rutland phoned with the name, we set our home-based people on it. But we didn't come up with much.'

41

'What did you come up with?'

Robson swung the chair slightly so that the afternoon sunshine touched his cheek, gave it colour and relieved it of its bloodlessness. 'Not a great deal. Conrad Gunther was born in Germany in 1915. He served in North Africa during the Second World War in the Panzer Corps. When the war was over, he went back to Germany for a few years but soon took the opportunity to leave. He travelled for a while but eventually ended up in South America. His solid war record found favour with German expatriates there – some of whom, no doubt, were ex-Nazis, though he is clearly not of that ilk – and he did well. He married the daughter of a diamond merchant in 1951, and he adopted a child two years later, a boy. Using capital left to his wife, he started a machine tools company which expanded with great speed. A successful businessman himself, he soon decided to go into consultancy. His machine tools factories he placed under a holding company, and he started his consultancy in South America, later South Africa and eventually Europe. He has done well, and continues to do well.'

He did not meet Crow's glance as the inspector asked quietly, 'So what was Rutland's interest in Gunther? He was hardly about to write of him in glowing terms. Was he going to suggest a Nazi background for him?'

Robson shook his head firmly.

'No chance of that. Conrad Gunther's record is impeccable. He was a soldier, not a Nazi; he had much in common with Rommel.'

'So what would have been Rutland's angle?'

Robson shifted uneasily in his seat. 'You have to realize, Inspector, in this game we work on whispers, rumour, even half-truths, which suddenly blossom into information that is ... something of a sensation. Rutland ... he felt that he could make use of a topical article on Gunther. You see, shortly, Gunther is coming to this country. It's said he will be talking about establishing a London HQ for his consultancy firm now that we are moving into Europe. He wants to forge links on that, and on machine tools in addition. You're aware, of course, that our machine tools industry is not in the healthiest of states. Gunther would be helping at top executive and Government level to right the matter. But Rutland–' he scratched his cheek nervously– 'Rutland thought we might embarrass Gunther, and the Government.'

'How?'

Robson did not reply immediately. He kept his eyes fixed on his desk. His mind was spinning, casting a web ahead, as he calculated chances and pressures and time. Gunther would be in England within ten days.

'I told you Gunther had set up in South Africa,' he said harshly. 'Well, Rutland had it on the grapevine that Gunther had used his agency there as a cover. He was carrying out trade agreements with Rhodesia. We felt that if we could prove this before Gunther arrived, we'd cause something of a sensation. You know – Government taking advice from an ex-enemy and a sanctions-breaker. It could have caused a flurry.'

There was a short silence. Crow sat still, watching Earl Robson's face.

'Is that the whole story?' he asked.

'Yes.'

At least, it's all you're going to bloody well get, Earl Robson thought viciously to himself.

When Crow had gone, Robson walked across to the liquor cabinet and poured himself a stiff whisky. He sipped it, staring into the mirror on the far wall. The colour had returned to his cheeks now, and his confidence had returned. No damned policeman was going to get the better of Earl Robson.

He took a stiff swallow and returned to his desk. He switched the intercom and called his secretary.

'I want Charlie Rutland's files brought up here immediately.'

They arrived ten minutes later. Over his second whisky Robson ploughed through them until he found the one he wanted. The file on Conrad Gunther.

If they moved quickly enough on this one, if someone else – young Grant perhaps – could dig up what Charlie suspected, they could still make it big – even tie in hints about Rutland's death.

He put down the file and walked across the room to the mirror. He stared at his reflection. There was a yellowish tinge about the whites of his eyes, as though he was suffering from some internal complaint. Or maybe it was nervousness. This story on Conrad Gunther–

The door whispered open behind him.

Robson spun on his heel, stupefied. No one came in here unannounced, his secretary vetted everyone first, and he opened his mouth in protest, but the man who had entered forestalled him.

'Good afternoon. I won't keep you long.'

He was young and tall and he moved with a slim, powerful grace. His fair hair was cut shorter than was the fashion among young men. There was a Slavic touch about his features and his eyes were pale blue, narrow, cold as the eyes of a snake. He was smiling, but his face was still and the smile meant nothing, formal as a stranger's handshake.

'Who the hell are you?' Robson demanded.

'My name is Dance.'

Incredibly, Robson saw him walk towards the desk. He glanced at the files spread out there and he picked up the one Robson had been studying. He turned to Robson, still smiling. 'I've come to collect these papers.'

Robson took a step forward, fluttered ineffectual hands in protest.

'But you can't come in here and–'

'I've come to collect these papers,' the stranger repeated, and the smile faded as his voice changed, took on an edge of menace. 'And to kill your story on Conrad Gunther.'

Chapter 4

1

Crow returned to Leeds on the morning train. The same policeman was on duty in the forecourt. Crow wondered whether he ever did anything else.

The police driver took him expertly through the morning traffic to the station headquarters. Wilson was waiting in the room set aside for them. He got straight down to business as soon as Crow arrived.

'I've spoken to Rutland's landlord. Not much he could tell me. He didn't like Rutland, though, and was a bit querulous about the suspicion that Rutland was subletting, of all things.'

'How do you mean?'

'It seems that shortly after Rutland took the bungalow the landlord was in the area and thought he saw someone go into the place. It wasn't Rutland and the landlord was a bit annoyed. He says it's clear enough from the lease that no subletting is allowed without his permission–'

'Was it a man or woman he saw going in?'

'A man. Apparently he went to the bungalow and knocked at the door but got no answer. He didn't have the keys on him so he left it then. But he complained to Rutland who denied he had a sublet – just said he'd allowed a friend to leave some fishing tackle there.'

Crow frowned.

'A friend? Any record of Rutland having a friend around here?'

'Can't trace anyone. So, either the landlord was mistaken, or Rutland was lying ... but subletting! Hardly in Rutland's line, I would have thought.'

'I'm inclined to agree. Anything else?'

Wilson nodded and pointed to a sheaf of papers on the desk. 'I instigated a thorough check with a number of the local men, and I soon came up with a few statements that have proved useful. Rutland visited a pub called the Three Bells during the last few weeks before he died. A couple of times he went there and back by taxi – other times he used the bus. The statements there on the desk are from a number of men who used the pub themselves, a taxi driver, and a couple of women who live near the Three Bells.'

'So what was the attraction of the Three Bells?'

Wilson's face was passive. 'The statements suggest it was a woman, the wife of the licensee.'

'And you think it's the woman?'

'If one can believe rumour.'

Crow grunted and reached for the statements. He read through them quickly. They displayed envy, malice, inquisitiveness in the affairs of other people. They amounted to little that was positive, but much that was customarily used by the police. It was a distasteful way of going about things, prying into people's lives by questioning their neighbours, but it had to be done. It was part of the job. Crow didn't like it. These would have to be followed up.

'Has anything come through from Dr Frust at forensic yet?' he asked, replacing the statements on the desk.

'Nothing so far. I've asked Detective-Sergeant Jones to call at the lab this afternoon and try to get them to hurry things along so we have an approximate time of death and so on. Frust did ring this morning before you came in and confirmed that the blood and hair on the poker is Rutland's and it is the murder weapon, but there was nothing by way of fingerprints that could be identifiable.'

Crow grimaced his dissatisfaction. 'Well, we'll need time of death before we can start pressing to conclusions on this,' he said, tapping the bunch of statements.

'I thought a preliminary interview might be useful, sir...'

'You've got the woman here?'

She had been waiting for an hour.

She was a big blonde woman with bedraggled eyes and a body that had seen good days and perhaps better nights. She was in her early thirties, but her flesh was beginning to spread, jowls had started to appear in her jawline and she sat heavy and solid in the chair. She was not unattractive; there was an overt sexuality about her, an animal warmth that would call many men and probably had. Crow preferred more subtle attractions, but he had no doubt that in a bar-room this woman would have had her fair share of attention. Her eyes brightened as she looked at him, walking into the room, as though she could hardly believe what she saw. Then the realization of his position rippled a nervous shudder through her and she looked away again.

Crow sat down, Wilson remained near

the door.

'Mrs Doris Orchard?'

'That's me,' she said, and made it sound defensive. Her voice had a throaty quality, sex or cigarette smoke, Crow couldn't decide.

'Do you know why you've been asked to come here?'

'No one told me nothing.' Sex. The throatiness had disappeared as sullenness intervened. It would come back.

'We want to have a talk with you about Charles Rutland.'

'Charlie–' Her mouth suddenly seemed ugly and tortured, as though she felt she didn't deserve her lot. 'I don't know nothing about that business.'

'You knew Rutland?'

'Of course. He used to come in the Three Bells for a drink. Started coming a month, six weeks back.'

'Did you get to know him very well?'

'I have a giggle and a chat with all the fellers who come in the bar,' she said swiftly, with the urgency of a woman seeking to forestall a question she didn't want to answer. 'It's good for trade, makes them think they're all Casanovas, that sort of thing. It doesn't mean anything, though. Bert–'

She stopped talking as quickly as she had started.

She stared at the floor. Her blonde hair was piled high, in a beehive hairdo. Stray pieces straggled away, and Crow could see her make-up had been carelessly applied this morning. Doris Orchard had things on her mind.

'What were you doing the night Rutland died?' Crow asked quietly.

'Working in the bar as usual.'

'Did you see Rutland in the bar that night?'

'I don't remember.'

But people always remembered seeing a person in such circumstances. Crow didn't say it, but it hung in the silence between them.

'We've got witnesses who say he was in the Three Bells on Friday night, Mrs Orchard.'

'Then I suppose he *was* there,' she said snappily. 'Friday, yes, he was there, I remember now, he was in the bar where I was serving and he was a bit cheeky, sort of familiar, you know, and I had to tell him not to take–'

'As far as I hear,' Crow interrupted, 'he was *always* rather familiar with you.'

The rhythm of her breathing changed. There was a hardness about her eyes as she looked at Crow. She tried to smile but its brilliance was forced.

'I told you, with *all* the men, I'm–'

'That's not the way we hear it,' Wilson interrupted. Crow leaned back in his chair and shook his head sympathetically.

'This isn't an attempt to trap you into admissions, Mrs Orchard. We have a number of statements here which say that you and Rutland were more than friendly. He was seen leaving the Three Bells several times, late at night, after closing time, when your husband was downstairs and you were not. We're not concerned about the situation over and above this one question: was Charles Rutland with you on the night he died?'

Doris Orchard shook her head vehemently. Then she sat, waiting. Crow and Wilson said nothing. She shifted in her chair and the silence deepened around her. She looked up, glancing from Crow to Wilson, and her eyes were dead. Slowly the colour ebbed from her face until her features seemed carved from chalk, high-lighted by smeared lipstick and dark eye-shadow.

'The hell with it,' she said dully. 'Yes. He was with me.'

'There is medical evidence to suggest he had sexual intercourse that evening.'

'Yes. I said it. He was with me.'

Crow leaned forward, elbows on the table. 'Perhaps you'd tell me about it – how long he's been coming to you, your husband's reaction–'

'Bert isn't my husband,' she said with a sudden tartness. 'I never been married, and Bert's got a wife in Southampton, he hasn't seen her in years. We been living together for five years, and at the Three Bells for three.' She paused and life flickered deeply in her eyes as though she were looking inward for the past. 'He had a pub in Birmingham and I worked in the bar. We decided to shack up together and he got the Three Bells.'

'And Rutland?' Crow prompted gently.

Doris Orchard shrugged indifferently. 'He showed up at the Three Bells a couple of months ago. Used to come in for a drink on a Friday, gave me the eye, chatted me up in the bar. He was interested. In the end, he used to visit me. He came about six or seven times in all.'

She anticipated Crow's next question. 'Bert wasn't bothered. You got to understand how it is. Bert and me are living together, but that don't give us any rights over each other. If he wants another woman, that's up to him. I don't think he does, actually, but that's up to him.' She hesitated, and defiance crept into her voice. 'Me, I'm different. I like men and Charlie Rutland showed he wanted me, so... And he was generous.'

'He gave you money?'

She bridled at the surprise in Crow's tone. 'It wasn't straight like that. He didn't have to give me money, but he chose to. It was a gift. That was all right by me. And Bert didn't mind, you understand that? *He didn't care.* It was all right by him. It was our arrangement.'

She lapsed into sudden silence and sat there, breathing heavily as though she had run a race. Her face was still white.

Crow was puzzled. Doris Orchard had made her admissions under very little pressure from him, and they were admissions a woman would not enjoy making. Yet he felt she was not telling him everything: she was giving, in an attempt to display candour, but it was a candour that concealed something else.

'Bert Orchard wasn't at the Three Bells?' he asked, looking towards the impassive Wilson.

'No, sir.'

'He went off to London yesterday,' Doris said hurriedly. 'Bert has to do all the buying for the pub, you know, cigarettes, cigars, crisps and all that. We been a bit fed up with the contracts some of the reps fixed for us, so Bert went down to sort things out.'

'That shouldn't take him long.'

'He's going to stay on for a week or so, take a holiday,' she said. 'Long time since he took a holiday. He's going to take a rest.'

'We'll want to talk to him. Where is he staying?'

'I don't know,' she said sullenly. 'He said he'd find a hotel and then ring me. He hasn't done it yet.'

Crow nodded as though satisfied and then addressed himself to Wilson.

'Put out a call to the Mets for Bert Orchard to be picked up. We'll want to talk to him.' Doris Orchard was glaring at him, her mouth open to protest, but Crow forestalled her. 'And we shall want to take a look around the Three Bells. Do you have any objection? If you do, I'll ask the inspector to swear out a search warrant.'

For a moment he thought she was going to argue, but the dullness came back over her eyes and she shook her head.

'All right,' Crow said quietly. 'Now tell me about the last time you saw Charles Rut-land.'

'She's lying, of course,' Wilson said emphatically after Doris Orchard had finished her statement and been allowed to leave. Crow stirred his tea thoughtfully and shrugged.

'In what way?'

'Well look how she was so quick to tell us about Rutland. She knew she had to give us something, to keep us happy. She knew there was enough gossip around to link her with Rutland so she admitted that. But she didn't tell us the whole story.'

Crow sipped his tea, pulled a face, reached for the sugar bowl and added another spoonful of sugar. It helped kill the bitterness of the long-standing canteen brew.

'I agree: she's keeping something back. We'll find out what it is when we get our hands on Bert Orchard.'

'It could be him.'

Crow was inclined to agree. The fact that the man was not available for questioning and Doris Orchard had been so evasive as to his whereabouts made it obvious he was to be regarded as a prime suspect.

'You think Bert Orchard was prepared to look the other way when she was with Rutland?' Crow asked. 'Seems a funny way to go on.' Wilson said, disapproval of such goings-on showing in his face. 'But it's possible.'

'Mmm.' Crow pushed away the tea, admitting defeat. 'I'm a bit puzzled about her and Rutland anyway ... I wouldn't have thought she was his type.'

'The slick journalist and the overblown barmaid. Maybe he just wanted an easy lay.'

'He certainly seems to have relaxed with her – maybe she was just that, relaxation from other things he had on his mind.'

Wilson turned in his chair to face Crow.

'I don't know we should pay too much attention to her story. She's trying to shield Bert Orchard, and maybe her talk about Rutland being *different* that evening could be just an attempt to cloud issues. Saying he was keyed up, excited, bothered, it could be a false trail to pull us away from Bert Orchard.'

'There are plenty of trails open to us,' Crow murmured. 'His managing editor, Earl Robson, reeled off a list of names of Rutland's enemies without even thinking about it.'

'I'll still settle for Bert Orchard,' Wilson said with a doggedness well known to Crow. He smiled and turned from the window. The light striking behind him emphasized his leanness and accentuated the hairless line of his skull.

'Yes, I want Bert Orchard too. And I want the Three Bells searched. Get it organized. As for Doris Orchard, we'll just accept Rutland was using her while he devoted his attentions to something important. Now, you've been to the bungalow – what about Rutland's possessions there?'

'I've got them in the other room, sir.'

2

They amounted to very little.

Charles Rutland had lived for the last few years in a flat in London but had accumulated few possessions. He had lived in a comfortable manner, and a perusal of his bank account suggested he had lived up to his salary. It had not been a munificent one, in spite of what Earl Robson had said: *Scathe* paid adequately but not tremendously well, probably because of the hidden overheads – particularly the threat of lawsuit.

It led Crow to the conclusion that Rutland worked for *Scathe* because he liked the sort of job he was called upon to do, ferreting out the secrets that their owners wanted to keep hidden. It was not the sort of job that

Crow would have liked; indeed, it was too near to the most distressing aspect of his own job to be comfortable. Crow was a professional, but that did not mean he enjoyed peeling away the veneers to disclose human frailties beneath.

Rutland's flat was still being searched and an inventory made of its contents, but the bungalow at Earston had not faced Detective-Inspector Wilson with a difficult problem. Rutland had few possessions in London; he had even fewer at Earston. It was quite obvious that he had never intended staying at the bungalow for any great length of time on any occasion. There were few items of clothing in the wardrobe in the bedroom. There were no books, no ornaments, no pictures – just the bare necessities, old furniture that had been rented with the bungalow, two bottles of whisky and one of brandy, five eggs, half a pound of bacon, a bottle of cooking oil and a box of tea bags.

'Hardly home from home,' Crow murmured as he read the list.

'It makes me wonder why he took the place,' Wilson said, and then gave a half-smile as he caught Crow's glance.

'You agree it wasn't love of Yorkshire, then?'

'He was working on a story, wasn't he?'

'And he rented the bungalow as a base, probably to save on hotel bills?'

'It still could have been a love of Yorkshire,' Wilson pondered heavily. 'There's a fine view from Earston Hill – you can see for miles.'

Crow grunted. 'We'll have to think about that one. All right, now let's have a look at this diary you found in his jacket.'

It was small, page-a-day, bound in red plastic. Inexpensive, it bore the appearance of regular use, the edges of the pages curling and grimed. Crow opened the diary. It was full of crabbed writing that made no sense to him.

'It looks to me as though it's a form of shorthand,' Wilson said. 'None of the accepted kinds, you know, but one that Rutland maybe worked out for himself.'

'There's none of it readable?'

'Not a thing – apart from the odd word. If you look at the back, though, you'll see he didn't always use the shorthand.'

Crow realized what Wilson meant. At the back of the diary Charles Rutland had kept brief notes of his expenses, with dates of the trips he had taken. The dates of his visits to West Berlin were there. No attempt had been made to use shorthand. Crow turned back in the diary to the dates of the German visit. The pages were crowded with notes, but they were all in Rutland's shorthand.

'This is more of annoyance value than anything else,' Crow said. 'We can get a cipher expert on it and it shouldn't be difficult to crack. The trouble is it takes time. And the results might be negative. Still, we'd better get it started.'

'You'll see from his expenses claims he made several visits up here after coming back from Germany,' Wilson said, 'before he ever got around to renting the bungalow.'

'I noticed. It may be we'll find the answer to that once the shorthand is transcribed.'

'There is another thing, sir.'

Crow raised his eyebrows interrogatively.

'Inside the front cover, sir.'

Crow opened the diary again. There were a number of words written there, scribbled in haste. Telephone numbers, hotel addresses, a name – Sandra Robson, followed by an address. Crow looked up.

'Have you checked all these?'

'The phone numbers are mainly business ones. The hotel addresses seem to have little significance. Sandra Robson–'

'Earl Robson's wife?'

'They were divorced some time ago.'

Crow considered the matter. Earl Robson did not like Rutland even though he had employed him. Rutland liked women, and he could have got to know Robson's wife easily enough.

'Get in touch with Carson at the Met,' he said decisively, 'and ask him to check on Mrs Robson. We'll want to know whether she knew Rutland well, and what Earl Robson thought about it. He's already got a list of people he's checking on; her movements during the last weeks might be of interest too. So ask Carson to add her to the list.' He shook his head. 'Robson told me it could be a long trail. Rutland wasn't exactly popular.'

'There is just one other thing,' Wilson added, pointing to the diary. 'This car number.'

'Rutland didn't drive. Could it be the number of the hire-car he used?'

'No, sir. I made a check on that – first thing that occurred to me. You'll see it's a Leeds number. Turns out it was a Volvo sports. The Leeds police were able to give me the details – where and when it was bought, year of manufacture and all that.'

'You mean they *had* the details?' Wilson nodded, frowning slightly.

'They did. You see, the car was reported stolen from a car park behind the Headrow, near the Merrion Centre.'

'Never recovered?'

'No.' Wilson hesitated. 'It didn't happen so long ago.'

'When was it taken?'

'It was reported stolen just three weeks ago.'

'And the car number goes into Charles Rutland's little red book,' Crow mused. 'Who owned the car?'

'It was reported stolen by a Mrs Aileen Selby. She lives at Selby Grange. It's a big house ... about two or three miles from Earston by road.'

'I think,' Crow said slowly, 'I'd better pay a call at Selby Grange.'

Chapter 5

1

It was all a question of patterns.

In any investigation such as this one, Crow saw the emergence of facts and relationships and events and characteristics as forming a series of kaleidoscopic patterns. One would be built up, but the appearance of a new factor would change the pattern and its colours: the redness of violence, the green of jealousy, the black of despair, anyone of these could touch the quality of a personal relationship and remould it until a new pattern appeared.

But at this stage it was too early to see patterns.

Crow stared out over the hazy moorland as the police car drove him towards Selby Grange, and he was hardly aware of the distant cooling towers of Huddersfield, the grey dotted sheep in their grey-walled compounds, industry and husbandry, the old past and the recent past. He was preoccupied with the confusions in his mind, the stubbornness of a picture that refused to become clear, the denial of a pattern of behaviour.

The journalist from *Scathe* magazine had come to Yorkshire and died there. He had formed a casual sexual relationship with a woman whose man had now gone south. Bert Orchard could have killed Rutland in a fit of rage, even though Doris said he didn't care. Sexual passion could be the motive.

But there was Robson too. He was a possessive, acquisitive, confident man: his confidence could have been shaken by the divorce his wife had won from him. Perhaps Rutland had had an affair with her, perhaps Robson had taken the chance to do something about it. A man could still want a woman he'd lost, still resent another using a possession that had once been his.

These were possible patterns, but there was also the question mark posed by a German businessman called Conrad Gunther. If Gunther was still on Rutland's mind when he died, for Crow the patterns were immediately disturbed, for a new factor was present. Was there any connection between Conrad Gunther and a village in Yorkshire, a bungalow in Earston?

Then there was a Volvo sports car stolen

from Leeds.

It could be an irrelevance, but its number was noted in Rutland's diary. Was there a connection between Rutland and Selby Grange?

Germany and Yorkshire, Gunther and Mrs Selby. Shifting patterns, shadows on a wall. The car sped over the hill and the sun broke briefly through the haze, so that the walled fields were grey-green and the gates to Selby Grange glittered in their white paint.

The gates were open and the car swept into the drive. Selby Grange lay three hundred yards ahead.

It was a nice house, a comfortable house. It had been built perhaps eighty years ago, Crow calculated, and was in a sense typical of the solidity of its builder: a man who would have seen profits come to him in middle age after years of hard work in the booming Yorkshire industries. From the mills had come the money that built homes like Selby Grange, not pretentious but practical, not flying too far from the sources of its wealth in either distance or attitude. Such men did not build follies, but homes.

Crow stood in the sitting-room and looked out through french windows to the grounds of the house. They would have been splendid once, but now the lawns were thick-edged and untidy, there was an air of decay and loss among the borders, and the trees had a bedraggled look as though conscious of better days.

The room in which he stood did not reflect such embarrassment. The furniture was hand-carved, cubes and oblongs, deep-cushioned and elegant. They formed a present which gave elegance to a past of dark oak floors and dark-beamed ceilings. The cream walls held original oil paintings in pale oak frames, the carpet was thick and deep. Expensive magazines made a casual litter on the marble-topped coffee table beside which Crow stood.

'Detective Chief Inspector Crow?' He turned and saw Aileen Selby.

She came through a breakfast-room that was sunlit and furnished in mahogany, and the light picked out her figure. He calculated she was almost fifty, but the tall elegance of her body would never admit it. She walked towards him, holding out a slim hand, and she moved with the grace of a model, the tranquillity of a cat, confident and assured.

She was dressed in black satin slacks of a casual cut and a white shirt. She was blonde, her short hair framing a face of classical lines. She was tall and small-breasted and her beauty was almost asexual, possessing a cold, controlled, clinical quality as firm and positive as her handshake.

'Please sit down,' she said, and took a seat herself, leaning back on one arm of the chair on the other side of the coffee table from him. 'I'm sorry you've been kept waiting.'

'Not at all,' Crow said in his gallant voice, the one which occasionally caused Martha such amusement. 'It gave me the opportunity to admire this room, and the view.'

Aileen Selby smiled. 'The room, yes, but the view... The cost of upkeep of gardens is prohibitive these days when a house like this has priority. My husband died almost ten years ago and he loved this house so much – it was built by his grandfather – but he would have been distressed to think I would have sold it. So, I retain it, even though it's something of a struggle. I think it's worth it.'

'I'd agree,' Crow said. 'Your husband was a local man, then.'

'Very much so. He never spent much more than a week away from his beloved Yorkshire. It's a lovely county, you know – the dales are magnificent, and even the towns have a harsh beauty of their own. He was a local man and he carried on in the family tradition. But the shoddy market declined, and when he died the business really died with him. When I sold it, I think a little of me died too.'

She said it lightly, dispelling any hint of sadness. 'You're not local, though,' Crow said.

She had green eyes that sparkled at him. 'I don't believe I ever came across an Australian who succeeded in eradicating the vowel sounds she heard as a youngster. I think it must be like an imprint on our vocal cords – and one completely irreversible. You're right, you detect an accent. Faint, I imagine, but it's there all right. I was born in Australia. I spent my youth there, came to England when I was twenty-five. I've lived up here in Yorkshire for more than twenty years now, though, so I ought to be counted a native.'

She looked out through the window briefly, as though searching for something, perhaps the sights and sounds of her child-hood, and then she turned back, smiling. 'My husband, John, he always thought of me as being more Yorkshire than he. And that's a compliment from a real native. But I'm chattering.' Her face grew serious and he noticed for the first time the lines around her eyes. They betrayed her age, gave testimony to her life experience. 'I suppose you've come about the car?'

'Not exactly.'

Calmly, she said, 'I didn't think it would be, exactly. I hardly imagined a detective chief inspector from Scotland Yard would be making enquiries about a stolen car alone. I imagine your primary task must be investigation of the Earston murder.'

Crow smiled. 'You're well informed, Mrs Selby.'

'Not really. It's just a matter of deduction. I know most of the senior people in the area, the Chief Constable and so on – and the name Crow does not figure among staff in this area. And I *have* read about the murder at Earston, just beyond the hill. This man named...'

'Rutland.'

'Yes, that's right. Well, it's a case of putting two and two together. But you know all about that.' She looked at him carefully, her head tilted a little to one side. 'What puzzles me is why you're *here*.'

'I'm a little puzzled myself.' Crow replied. 'Can you explain why the number of your car – the stolen car – should have been of interest to Charles Rutland? We found it noted in his diary.'

Aileen Selby frowned. 'Er ... I did ask the maid to bring in some tea. Will that be acceptable? Good. Now then, my car number and Rutland. I can't imagine...'

'Did you ever meet Rutland?'

She registered alarm tinged with a certain amusement. 'Not consciously, I assure you. From what I read in the papers he was a journalist of dubious calibre, wasn't he? I suppose there's the *possibility* that I might have seen him in Earston village when I've been there, but as I say, not *consciously.*'

Crow began to speak, but the maid entered from the breakfast-room with a silver tea-service. He waited until she had gone, and watched as Aileen Selby poured tea into two delicate china cups. When he took the tiny cup and saucer from her, they looked ridiculous in his long bony fingers.

'Is it all right, Inspector? Now then, where were we?'

'You told me you were not aware that you had ever met Charles Rutland.'

She nodded, and he caught the gleam of silver among the blondeness of her hair. It surprised him: he had assumed the colour was not natural.

'No, I can't think I ever did meet him. And

I certainly have no idea why he should have noted the Volvo number in his diary.'

Crow sipped his tea, feeling gauche and awkward. At home he had a favourite mug, and Martha used a homely brown pot to brew the tea. A silver tea-service and delicate china looked fine but– He broke away from the thought.

'Tell me about the car. What exactly happened?'

'It's quite simply told, really.' She frowned slightly as though annoyed with herself, chiding herself for her carelessness. 'I could have sworn I locked it … I'd gone to Leeds to do some shopping and I parked at the Merrion Centre. I'd left the ticket in the car, so whoever took the Volvo had to pay the parking fee. Cheap at the price, wasn't it!'

'How long were you away from the car?'

'Not more than two hours. But I feel sure I *did* lock it – the police told me they guessed it must have been a professional thief. The car was valuable, naturally, but worse than that was the fact it was a present to me from my future son-in-law. I panicked, of course, when I realized the car was gone, and I phoned the police immediately. But … nothing.'

'If it was a professional thief, I doubt if

you'll see it again. Settle for the insurance.'

'But that's not the same thing, is it?' She hesitated, eyeing Crow carefully. 'As for this Rutland thing ... do you think *he* might have stolen the car?'

Crow had the odd impression that his answer was important to her. He shook his head. 'There's nothing to suggest that he did – and I've no idea why he wrote the number in his diary. I'd hoped–'

When he paused she raised her chin. 'Yes?'

'Nothing. It doesn't look as though you'll be able to help. I'm sorry I've had to bother you, Mrs Selby. I regret taking up so much of your time. I'll be on my way–'

'Nonsense,' Aileen Selby said firmly. 'It's all rather exciting, really. Do have another cup of tea. Visitors are not numerous to Selby Grange, and certainly not Scotland Yard chief inspectors.'

She looked at him suddenly as though she were noting his unprepossessing appearance for the first time. He found the glance disturbing; it was as though she had been too tense or too preoccupied earlier to take stock of him physically. Yet he had thought her completely at ease. It made him wonder now whether there was more to Aileen Selby than he might have realized.

'Tell me about Charles Rutland,' she said in a voice slightly lowered for confidences. She leaned forward as she spoke, and injected excitement into her green eyes. 'After all, it isn't every day a murder takes place on one's doorstep.'

'Earston's three miles away – hardly your doorstep,' Crow said, a little embarrassed.

'Three miles by road, not a mile as the crow–' She stopped short and smiled. 'Oh dear.'

Crow laughed. 'I have been told my methods can be pretty direct, too,' he said.

'How successful are they in the Rutland case?' she asked, still smiling, but he brushed the question aside.

'It's too early to say. There are a few ... enquiries to be made. But I *have* taken up too much of your time.'

'Not at all.'

She sat staring at the coffee table while Crow finished the cup of tea, and then, as he began to rise to his feet, she looked up and gave him a brilliant smile.

'I'm sorry I've been of so little assistance.'

'There are many enquiries in a case like this which will lead nowhere. I'm only sorry you've been bothered.'

She smiled again, rose and walked ahead

of him towards the door. He noted the grace of her bearing once more as she moved across the hallway, and it made him more conscious of his own height and awkwardness.

At the door she hesitated, and almost in spite of herself she said, 'Do you have *any* idea as to who might have murdered this man Rutland?'

2

Crow had long accustomed himself to the necessity of making snap judgments about people. It was true that many of his judgments were redeemed later, but it was equally true that many of his judgments proved erroneous. Yet he felt his judgment of Aileen Selby had been accurate. She was a cool, self-possessed woman of character, and yet now, as he half smiled and shook his head reluctantly, she said, 'I suppose you think I'm a gossiping woman, full of feminine and foolish curiosity.'

It was the last category Crow would have placed her in, and yet she was affecting coyness in a disturbing way; disturbing because coyness and curiosity were not normal factors in her make-up.

'It's not that, Mrs Selby,' Crow replied. 'These are early days, and lines of enquiry haven't hardened yet. For instance, there's no reason to assume that your car is in any way connected with Rutland's murder. The car number in his diary – that's puzzling, but not necessarily linked–'

He stopped speaking as he heard a voice outside the door. Next moment he was forced to step aside hurriedly as the door was flung open, and Mrs Selby also had to move quickly, to avoid being struck by the door.

'Oh – Mother! I'm sorry–'

A young girl stood in the doorway, half laughing but yet expressing a certain consternation that she had entered the house so violently as almost to strike the two people leaving it. Crow stared at her as she put a hand out to her mother. She was a younger edition of Aileen Selby; shorter by an inch or so, freer, lighter of temperament, possibly more at ease than her mother. There was a softness about her that suggested she had been untouched by the harsh reality of living, in the way her mother would have been. Crow caught the glance Aileen Selby bestowed on her daughter and guessed she never would be so touched, if Mrs Selby had her way. Love and pride glowed out of Aileen Selby's eyes.

'You won't have met Detective Chief Inspector Crow.' Aileen Selby said with a hint of mockery. Then, as the girl swung around, wide-eyed, she added, 'This is my only daughter Ingrid.'

Ingrid Selby held out a slim hand. 'Detective Chief Inspector! Gosh! I bet you're working on that murder over at Earston! How exciting! You got any clues yet? Any idea who might have done it? It's not often we get a murder around here, believe me, and it's had the whole place buzzing!'

Crow shook hands with the girl and glanced wryly at Mrs Selby. 'I came to see your mother about another matter in fact, and was just on my way. I've no doubt she'll tell you all about it, Miss Selby.'

A shadow of disappointment touched the girl's features. 'The car, I suppose. You've come about the Volvo. That's not half so exciting – though I suppose it's the only crime we've come into contact with. Have you found it?'

'Ingrid–' Mrs Selby began.

'We haven't found it,' Crow said. 'But the man murdered at Earston had its number in his diary.'

'You mean *he* might have stolen it?'

She wriggled involuntarily. Her eyes were as green as her mother's, but sparkling in their depths with sudden excitement. Crow shook his head.

'We don't know that, miss. But ... I don't suppose you can suggest any reason why the dead man might have taken a note of the car number? I mean, did you ever–'

Aileen Selby moved forward, almost placing herself between her daughter and Crow as she rested one hand casually upon Ingrid's shoulder in a gesture at once possessive, loving and defensive.

'Ingrid is hardly able to give you an answer to any question you ask about Rutland or even Yorkshire, for that matter. She couldn't ever have seen him – there's hardly a soul around here she knows at all. She's spent little time in Yorkshire of recent years – and in the last six months I've seen her only for a matter of weeks.'

Ingrid slipped her arm around her mother's slim waist, gave her an affectionate squeeze. From a distance they might have seemed twins but for the contrast between the older woman's cool elegance and the younger's barely suppressed excitement at life. Mother looked affectionately at daughter.

'Not that I object in any way,' she said quietly. 'You'll see lots of us, Mother! I know you've been nervous and upset these last few weeks–'

Aileen Selby interrupted her with a quick laugh, looking towards Crow.

'Who wouldn't be nervous, with a big wedding in the offing! That car, Inspector, I believe I told you it was a present from my prospective son-in-law. Chris and Ingrid are to be married shortly. She's just been spending a few days here, finalizing everything before we fly off for the wedding. And the nearer it's got, the more nervous I've become.'

Crow would have thought her far too controlled a person to display nervousness over wedding plans.

'Where will the wedding take place?'

'In Crete,' Aileen Selby replied. 'And on a boat! Really, I–'

'It's a yacht,' the girl said firmly, 'not a boat. And it's going to be marvellous. Imagine, Inspector–'

Aileen Selby pushed her gently aside, smiling. 'I'm sure Inspector Crow is not interested in your wedding plans.' She turned her full green gaze on Crow. 'Again, I'm sorry I can't help you more.'

The interview was over. Crow went down the steps to the police car, noting the yellow, powerful sports car parked a few feet behind it. Another present from the prospective son-in-law, he guessed, but this time to the prospective bride.

He spent little time over the thought. As the police car took him back over the moors to the hotel HQ at Backchapel, he was hardly aware of the sunshine filtering through the smoky mirk of distant chimneys. He was thinking about cool, self-possessed women and the effect a policeman could have upon them.

He had added to his store of experience today. His presence and questions had made Aileen Selby try to appear a gossip and an empty, curious woman. She was neither. Yet she'd wanted to give him that impression – and she hadn't wanted him to talk to her daughter.

It could be that she was over-protective. Or it could be she had something to hide.

3

The menu boasted roast duck a l'orange.

Crow generally avoided duck, which he found too fatty for his tastes, although Martha always chose duck on the rare occasions they went out to dine together. He was all but forced to choose it this evening, however, since the proprietor, Joe Bembridge, insisted it was a speciality of the house.

It was.

As he ate, Crow regretted that his wife was not with him. She would have enjoyed this duck. He suddenly resented Wilson's presence and glowered at him. Wilson looked surprised.

'How's your duck?'

'Fine,' Crow grunted reluctantly.

'I thought–' Wilson decided not to give vent to his thoughts.

Crow was sorry for his surliness. It wasn't Wilson's fault after all that Crow was parked out here in the wilds of Yorkshire when he could have been among the comforts of home with his wife.

'More wine?'

Wilson nodded, and watched while Crow poured the glass of wine for him. His cheeks were already a little flushed.

'I sent the diary off to York this afternoon,' he said. 'There's a Ministry of Defence cipher expert over there. They reckon he's a crack. Should sort it out quickly enough. Then we'll know what My Charlie Rutland has been up to.'

'Nothing on this man Orchard yet?' Crow asked.

'No. There's a general call out. I got hold of Carson at the Met, though, as you said.' Wilson sipped his wine appreciatively. 'He rang me back just before I left Leeds. It's as we guessed about Robson.'

'How do you mean?'

'Earl Robson, editor of *Scathe* magazine, was not above getting involved in scandal himself. Divorced for adultery, wife cited four women. But Robson didn't like losing her. Robson, it would seem, even put a tail on her.'

'Where did this information come from?'

'It was on file,' Wilson replied. 'I understand the ex-Mrs Robson made a complaint to the police that she was being followed. It was never taken up more than that – but there's a suspicion that Rutland was seeing the woman.'

'After the divorce, you mean?'

'Yes, sir. And Robson didn't like it.'

'I wonder how *much* he didn't like it.' Crow said thoughtfully.

They finished the meal, each concerned

with his own thoughts. Joe Bembridge, a big, florid man with a smiling face, came across to ask them how they'd enjoyed their meal, and Crow expressed enthusiasm. To Wilson's surprise and Bembridge's pleasure, he suggested that Bembridge and his wife join them for coffee.

'It will give me the opportunity to compliment the lady cook,' Crow said gallantly.

Bembridge went out to make sure the bars were staffed in his absence and then returned with his wife. In some ways she reminded Crow of Martha: she was of the same height, and possessed the comfortable roundness that middle-aged women often accepted where younger ones fought it off. Crow liked her, for her button eyes and cheerful smile. When he congratulated her upon the meal, her wary shyness evaporated and she forgot Crow's appearance and took him for what he was.

They chatted over coffee, and at last Crow said casually, 'I was up at Selby Grange this afternoon. I met Mrs Selby and her daughter.'

'Nice people,' Mrs Bembridge said. 'Monied, but no side with them, no sticking noses in the air. Nice people.'

'She's Australian, I gather – Mrs Selby.'

'That's right. Far as I remember, from what I heard at the time, she came over at the end of the war. They tell me she had a broken marriage out there, or her husband was killed or some suchlike, and she came over, got a job in the office in John Selby's shoddy works and ... well, there it was. She made good, married the boss.'

'I understand Selby died a few years back.'

'That's so,' Joe Bembridge said. 'His grandfather built up a small business in shoddy, but it was John Selby who really made it pay. But in a sort of way he worked hisself out. Died before he was retirin' age. Hard, that, but there's nowt a chap can do about it. Still, he'd have been proud to see the way his daughter's growed. And Mrs Selby brought her up right, no doubt about that.'

'It wasn't too easy for her, either,' Mrs Bembridge added. 'They had brass, of course, but less than many folk supposed – she had to sell up the firm–'

'That was because of that accountant,' her husband interrupted. 'Got put away for ten years, embezzlement, they said, but it left Mrs Selby in a bit of trouble.'

'So she sold up.' Crow offered the coffee-pot in Mrs Bembridge's direction. 'More coffee?' As he poured he said, 'I got the impression from the house that it had all seen better days. Mrs Selby herself, though, she's still a very attractive woman.'

'She is that,' Mrs Bembridge said with candour. 'There was a bit of talk in fact, year or so back – a chap called Harry Field, in Bradford, was keen on her. An Australian feller who knew her when she was a slip of a girl, they say. Wanted to marry her but she turned him down. Maybe she thought he wouldn't be the right kind of father for her girl.'

'She dotes on her, sure enough,' Joe Bembridge agreed. 'You ... er ... you weren't up at the Grange about the murder, were you?'

Crow smiled and shook his head. 'No, I was just making enquiries about their car, the one that was stolen. But I met Ingrid Selby while I was there. I understand she's to be married soon.'

Mrs Bembridge reacted enthusiastically as many women do to the thought of marriage. 'That's so, and it shows what I meant, and what Joe said about bringing the girl up right. Mrs Selby did the best for Ingrid, sent her to good schools – I mean, if she hadn't sent her to the finishing school in Scotland, where she learned to ski, she wouldn't have met Chris Santer, would she? So it paid off, didn't it?'

'You mean Mrs Selby regarded it as an investment?' Crow said, laughing. Mrs Bembridge laughed too, but her husband nodded sagely.

'Ah, well, it depends what you mean by investment. Good education, good school, good marriage. Chris Santer ... that young chap'll have more brass than I'll ever see in two lifetimes when he follows his father. Alfred Santer made a fortune they say, in biscuits, and he started small enough in Scotland. But the old man hasn't got long to live. He's had two heart attacks recently, and when he dies young Chris Santer will take over. Oh aye, it were a good investment Mrs Selby made, sending Ingrid to that school in Scotland. Not that she'd have known Ingrid would have met Chris Santer, of course.' He turned his head and twinkled a smile at his wife. 'Though if she's like some women I know, I wouldn't put it past her to have known. Do you find women are like that, Inspector Crow? Cunning as a barrelful of monkeys.'

Mrs Bembridge reacted indignantly at her husband's teasing, but Crow said nothing. He was still thinking about Aileen Selby. She had got the best for her daughter, and

she was the kind of woman who would want
to keep it.

But there was nothing wrong with that.

Chapter 6

1

The Chief Constable was a large, homely, untidy man with sandy hair and almost invisible eyelashes. He had a sensitive mouth which reflected his feelings. There would have been occasions when he would have been exposed by that mouth, but now it was smiling quizzically as the Chief Constable leaned back in his chair and observed John Crow.

'I hear you've been out to see Aileen Selby.'

'That's right.'

'About her car. I shouldn't think she'll have been able to tell you much about why its number was in Rutland's diary. I know her vaguely – know of her, certainly. A friend of mine – Harry Field – he's in the wool business in Bradford, he surprised us all by proposing to her a year or so back. She turned him down. But he knew her as a young woman. Born about 1925 in Alice Springs, came to England in her mid-twenties, got a job in John Selby's shoddy works, married him in 1951, Ingrid Selby born in 1953...' He paused, smiled wryly. 'It gets to be a habit, doesn't it, keeping tabs on other people's lives. I dredged it all up out of the back of my mind, after I heard you were out there. Couldn't think why you were going there, until I heard about the diary entry.'

'News travels fast.'

A tremor of consternation touched the Chief Constable's mouth. 'Not gossip. It's just that the liaison officer–'

Liaised, Crow thought grimly as the Chief Constable let the words die. He'd have to speak to Jones, explain to him the duty of silence. The Chief Constable coughed gently. 'As a matter of fact, Jones raised the matter of the missing Volvo with us. He asked for the file.'

'It's with Detective-Inspector Wilson at the moment,' Crow said.

'Well, I hope he can make more of it than we were able to,' the Chief Constable said, twisting in his chair uncomfortably. 'The fact is, from the moment that car was taken from the Merrion Centre it seems to have vanished into thin air. We suspect it was a professional thief: an expensive car, taken from a car park, with the thief paying the parking fee and driving off cool as you like! I suppose it ended up in some garage with a bent mechanic stripping it, respraying it, changing the plates and selling it to some unsuspecting member of the public.'

'That doesn't explain why Rutland was interested in it.'

'What does?' The Chief Constable gave Crow a quick, stabbing look. 'That'll be your problem. We worked on one other theory at the time – we checked on reports of petty crime and robbery in the whole of the area, to discover whether the Volvo might have been used as a getaway car.'

'No luck?'

'None.' The Chief Constable's mouth expressed dissatisfaction. 'We did have a wave of break-ins at about that time and we did some enquiring, but the Volvo didn't turn up. We wondered at one point whether a report about a foreigner up at the Three Bells had anything to do with it–'

'Excuse me. A foreigner?'

The Chief Constable raised a placatory hand. 'All right, I know, it's a bit far fetched. A car of foreign make stolen, so we wonder about a foreigner seen in the area! It seemed a good idea to follow it up at the time.'

Crow leaned forward, elbows on his bony knees. 'No, you miss my point. You say there was a foreigner at the Three Bells?'

The Chief Constable frowned. His eyes took on an inward look as though he was seeking the past within himself.

'Now let me think back. Probably about a month ago, or thereabouts. I told you, we'd had a wave of break-ins, and one of our plainclothes division was up at the Three Bells when he saw this foreigner. He made some enquiries of the licensee, Orchard, and learned the man had booked a room for the night. He checked out next day and that was that – he wasn't seen again. Didn't come back to mind until the Volvo was taken and one of the lads thought he'd check it out. Got nowhere.'

'When you say "foreigner", what exactly do you mean? Yorkshire foreign?'

The Chief Constable chuckled. 'I didn't take up the point with the lads, but as I understood them they meant not *British*. Beyond that...' He shrugged. 'As far as I remember he'd registered in a Russian name, but hadn't entered his nationality. The Orchards don't seem to have been too fussy about the state of their registers.' His mouth drooped. 'Don't suppose any of this is relevant, though. We never saw hide nor hair of the chap afterwards, and it may be he wasn't connected at all with the Volvo theft. No reason why he should have been, really.' He glanced at his watch suddenly and grimaced. 'However, I've an appointment with the Chairman of the Bench in forty minutes. You'll be waiting for this chap Savil, I suppose.'

'The hire-car driver? Yes. I understand they've contacted him and are bringing him in today.'

The Chief Constable consulted his watch again. 'Should be here any moment now. I'll be on my way, Crow. There's a room at your disposal along the corridor. You'll keep in touch?'

Crow nodded. 'I shall keep you informed of developments, sir.'

They both knew what that meant: Crow would tell the Chief Constable as much as Crow felt he should know and no more. The courtesies had been extended, however, and the Chief Constable could go on his way, satisfied, to his appointment. Crow left him in the corridor and made his way to the room set aside for his use. The liaison officer, Detective-Sergeant Jones, was already there. Crow thought about raising the gossip issue with him, but decided against it: there was no point in starting antagonisms at this stage. Jones's servility irritated Crow nevertheless, and he soon sent the man to get him some coffee.

Crow stared out of the window. The yard below him was empty; the hill outside the gateway stretched down past a huddle of squat, ugly offices that had once been double-fronted houses.

The towns have a harsh beauty of their own, Mrs Selby had said. Crow didn't see it. They were dark, dirty, depressing even in sunlight. He wouldn't say so to Wilson: the Yorkshireman would never forgive him.

A police car came up the hill and turned into the gateway, indicator flashing. Two policemen got out; they were followed by a stocky man in a flat cap and leather jacket.

Savil had arrived.

2

His hair was long, his eyes offended, his temper thin. The moustache he sported threatened to take over his face; it should have added strength to his jaw, but it merely gave his features a bedraggled expression, as though he was overcome by facing a problem that would not go away.

'I was on holiday.'

He said it belligerently, but the moustache changed the belligerence to uncertainty, and the doubts peeped out of his flat eyes to keep his tone company.

'Lake District,' he added, and the belligerency had gone completely to be replaced with an aggrieved air. Crow sympathized; he had often enough been dragged back from leave to work on a Murder Squad case.

'We've spent some time trying to contact you, Mr Savil. It was important.'

'About this chap Rutland, I suppose.' Savil chewed the end of his moustache thoughtfully. 'Seen about it in the paper, but I didn't think you'd want to talk to me. Don't see what I can do to help.'

'You must understand,' Crow said, 'in a case of murder we have to follow all lines of enquiry. One thing that's been puzzling us is what Rutland was doing in this area.'

'Liked the country, didn't he?'

Rutland obviously commanded Savil's respect for that much at least. Crow regarded him for a moment, and said, 'That's why he was here? As a tourist?'

Savil shrugged. 'I always thought so. He

did enough driving around, I'll say that, even though it wasn't exactly always the beauty spots he wanted to see. Meself, I always think Wharfedale–'

'Did he explain his ... er ... tours as sightseeing?'

'He never did any explaining.' Savil touched his straggly moustache gingerly, as though checking to make sure it was still there. 'I mean, I didn't ask, he didn't offer. As far as I was concerned, as long as he paid for what was on the clock I couldn't care less.'

'And he did a lot of moving around?'

'He did that.'

'What impression did you have about all this?' Crow asked. 'I mean, did he appear to be looking for something, or was it strictly sightseeing?'

Savil looked vaguely puzzled. 'Don't quite know what you mean. After all, he was paying to be driven around, so I drove him.'

Crow frowned. The interview was unproductive so far; Savil seemed to have been completely uninterested in Charles Rutland, and his curiosity would seem to have been nonexistent. His eyes had been only for the mileage clock.

'Did you use to pick up Rutland at his bungalow?'

'Most times I did, yes, that's right.'

'Was he always alone there?'

A little of the earlier belligerence crept back into Savil's tone as he replied, 'Hell, I don't know. I never saw anyone there but him. But I'm no snoop, you know. I was just being paid–'

'To drive him and you did that. Yes, I get the picture. Have you got a record of the trips he took with you?'

Savil nodded. He reached in his jacket for a small pocketbook that he consulted briefly, riffling through the pages. 'Most of them are here. I try to keep it down like this so I don't get no arguments with the tax inspector. I tell you, being self-employed–'

'I'd be grateful,' Crow interrupted smoothly, 'if you could let us have a look at that book for a while.'

Savil hesitated, tapping the book against his thumb. 'Suppose so. Won't do any harm, but I want it back. You'll see where I took him, with the mileages, except for the last few times. My holiday was coming up and I got a bit careless about keeping the book up to date.'

He handed the book to Crow, explaining that the trips taken with Rutland were marked CR – the dead man's initials. Crow looked quickly through the dates prior to Rutland's death. The pages were blank. He turned over several pages and then frowned. 'CR. You've got those initials marked on a page for April twelfth.'

'So?'

Crow looked up slowly. 'I was under the impression you drove him around only during June.'

Savil's eyes reflected his indifference. 'Can't help about your impressions, mate. If it's down there for April twelve, so it was. The tax inspector–'

'Let's get this clear. You drove Rutland around before June. How often?'

'It's there in the book. You check through it, you'll see. Dates and places. No need for me–'

'Tell me about it all the same,' Crow interrupted. 'Was April the twelfth the first occasion?'

Savil wrinkled his nose in thought and bared his teeth to nibble at his moustache. It obviously helped his memory. He nodded vigorously. 'Right. That was the first time. Twelfth and thirteenth. Then I didn't see him again for a while. Check it in the book, but I reckon it must have been around about May tenth. Pretty sure of that because it was my Aunt Mabel's birthday and I was able to drop in for a quick nip on the way back home that day. While Mr Rutland was in the pub, that is.'

'Pub? What pub?'

'The Three Bells, of course! Mabel lives not two blocks from there. We'd been up above Menstone and we stopped back at the Three Bells. Rutland said he was going in for a drink and would I wait outside, so I said the hell with that, I'd visit my aunt and I did.' He glared angrily at Crow. 'I wasn't sitting in the bloody car while he sank a few in the warm.'

The Three Bells. It seemed to be figuring at several turns in the last days of Charles Rutland. Crow turned the pages of the pocketbook. 'Was that the only time you took him there?'

'Hell, no. We called there on April twelve and thirteen, but the tenth was the last time, tenth of May, that is.' He scowled at the thought. 'I did hear he went there often enough during June. There was talk ... but he was using a bus, I reckon, there and back.'

Crow was puzzled. With the pocketbook in front of him, he opened the file at his elbow and began to compare some of the dates Wilson had copied from Rutland's own diary. On April 10 Charles Rutland had returned from Germany and would seem to have gone to Yorkshire. On April 12 and 13 Savil had driven him around Menstone, and on one of those days he had stopped at the Three Bells.

Savil had not seen Rutland again until the tenth of May: Rutland's own diary showed he had returned to Germany during the intervening period – presumably checking on the Conrad Gunther story. He had gone to the Three Bells on the tenth.

'What was Rutland doing on your earlier trips?' Crow asked.

Savil sniffed. 'Looking around a bit, visitin' places for rent and so on.'

'And when did you see him after the tenth of May?'

'Several times in June – between the fifth and fifteenth. He'd rented that bungalow by then. On the twenty-fifth I went on holiday. He said it didn't matter, he wouldn't be needing me.'

'Nor did he,' Crow said softly. 'He died next day.'

Something happened to Savil's face; the colour left it, and his whole personality seemed to retreat from the softness of Crow's voice. He opened his mouth as though he needed more air. 'What you tryin' to say?'

Crow shook his head. He was puzzled. A

trip to Germany, a visit to the Three Bells, return to Germany after seeking a bungalow, a rental, and then a gap until June 5 when Savil started calling at the bungalow to take Rutland for drives out into the country. Places and mileages were checkable, but what was Rutland doing, driving around in a seemingly aimless fashion?

Savil provided no answer. He was no more interested now than then. His mind was clearly on his fishing, and he wanted to return to his holiday. Finally, Crow allowed him to leave, after getting an address where he could be easily contacted.

After Savil had gone, Crow spent the next hour or so poring over the pocketbook and the dates Wilson had noted down from Rutland's diary. At last he asked Jones to bring in a large-scale map of the area. It was pinned up on the wall, and, as Crow called out the place names, Jones flagged them on the map.

'What was the last place Savil mentioned – the one he hadn't noted in this pocketbook?' Crow asked.

'Bleak Hey,' Jones replied.

'Flag it,' Crow said, and sat staring at the map. Charlie Rutland certainly had done his share of travelling during June. But as Crow stared at the map, he could discern no pattern to it. The trips were not based on the Three Bells; they formed no logical outward run; they visited areas of beauty and harshness alike; they seemed to have nothing in common. But Rutland had had a reason for making them.

At last, disgruntled and disappointed, Crow went to the canteen for a cup of tea. He sat alone, hardly aware of the covertly curious glances that some of the local policemen indulged in. He was immersed in his problems, trying to see where all these disparate facts led. The outcome had been a vicious killing, but Crow could not yet trace the intervening steps.

Orchard, Robson, even Gunther might provide an answer.

When he left the canteen and walked back towards the operations room, there was a young constable walking ahead of him. He was not aware of Crow, and, as he drew alongside the open door of the room Crow used, he looked inside, saw Jones, called his name and went in. When Crow entered quietly, the young constable was standing with his hands on his hips, beside Jones, staring at the flagged board.

'Hey, you're after the bastard too, are you?' he was saying with a smile in his voice.

'What's he done now, then?'

'Who?'

At the sound of Crow's voice the constable whirled in consternation, and Jones also looked flustered.

'I'm sorry, sir,' the constable said, turning a little pink. 'I didn't realize you were behind me.'

'That's all right, nothing wrong... You were displaying a certain interest in that flagged map?'

The constable became even pinker. 'Only because I've done those rounds myself, sir, only last year. I was on patrols then, and we went chasing up to most of those places. I was just thinking, you must be after him too and–'

Patiently, Crow interrupted him. 'After who?'

The constable blinked, glanced uncertainly at Jones, took another swift look at the map and licked his lips nervously. 'Why...' He hesitated and his blue eyes widened. 'Why, Shuffler, isn't it?'

3

'Who is Shuffler?'

103

The Chief Constable scratched his sandy hair, inspected his fingernail briefly and then shrugged. 'Shuffler is an itinerant, a knight of the road. He's been hanging around the Yorkshire dales as long as anyone can remember. During the winter months he usually manages to make a nuisance of himself around the Leeds and Bradford areas, sometimes get locked inside for vagrancy, petty theft, that sort of thing, though I suspect all he's really looking for is a roof over his head. He's harmless enough, and some of the chaps even have a sort of affection for him. He's a difficult customer in the sense he's damned independent in many ways. Won't give tuppence for a copper, so to speak.'

'You were looking for him last year,' Crow said.

The Chief Constable nodded. 'There was an outbreak of arson in the town. There's never been any suggestion in the past that Shuffler was that way inclined, but at one of the fires a report was handed in that someone answering Shuffler's description was seen running away from the mill just before the fire must have started. So, we looked for him. Merry dance he led us, too.'

'You've a description of him?' Crow asked.

The Chief Constable laughed and his

mouth was generous in its displayed amusement. He showed broad, tombstone teeth. 'You don't need a description of Shuffler. You can *smell* him before you see him. Believe me, when we've had him inside it's taken three days of bathing to get even the top layers of dirt off him. It's hell's own job to get him to take his clothes off.' The Chief Constable shook his head. 'Still, if you want a description he's about four ten in his stockinged feet, no more than that. Tiny little feller. Bald as a billiard ball...'

He was unable to restrain himself; his eyes strayed to Crow's own gleaming skull and sudden embarrassment twitched his mouth out of shape. Hurriedly, he went on, 'It looks incongruous because he doesn't shave and the lower part of his face is covered with a beard as matted as a bird's nest. Last time he was here he was wearing the same old pinstripe he's worn for twenty years, and a pair of worn-out gumboots. He keeps a leather belt strapped around his waist, and there's a collection of pans and cans that dangle from it, make a hell of a racket.'

The Chief Constable inspected his fingernail again and picked away from it dandruff that had lodged under the nail. 'I've heard it suggested he's not short of a few bob. Keeps it in one of the cans ... but when we've pulled him in there's been nothing in the bloody cans but dirt and grease.' He rubbed his fingernail against his jacket with a vigorous polishing motion.

'Did the arson charge reach him?' Crow asked.

'Hell, no. That was a waste of public money, chasing over the county looking for him. We got the arsonist a few weeks later; Shuffler was clean – figuratively speaking. But we had a hell of a job finding him. I had a patrol car visiting all his known haunts: he's got eight or nine places where he holes up during the summer–'

'And one of those would be Bleak Hey,' Crow said. The Chief Constable blinked his invisible eyelashes and regarded Crow with an open curiosity. 'What's all this about?' he asked.

Crow explained. 'When Charles Rutland came back up here in June, he used Savil to drive around quite a bit. From Savil's pocket-book we've been able to flag a map of the places Rutland visited. One of your constables saw the flagged map and tells me that those places by and large match up with the sites he visited last year, looking for this tramp, Shuffler. Is that the only name you know him by?'

The Chief Constable nodded. His brow was puzzled. 'Are you suggesting Rutland was looking for Shuffler? What the hell would he want with him? I can't see our Shuffler coming up with any useful material for a journalist of Rutland's kind, and Shuffler himself has no life story to tell: the only things he's slept with are lice.'

'Well, I shall have to follow it up, anyway. I'll need a couple of men who know these areas well, so that if he does prove difficult to find we'll be able to root him out. It may be he's still at Bleak Hey–'

'I doubt it,' the Chief Constable said with a grunt. 'But you can certainly have a couple of men and a patrol car. Even so, I can't imagine what the hell Rutland would have–'

The telephone on the Chief Constable's desk jangled, and he picked it up with the air of a man ruled by the instrument. The conversation was entirely one way, after an acknowledgment of identity by the Chief Constable. Crow waited as the Chief Constable listened, and then looked up as the phone was replaced.

'You could have taken that as well as I,' the Chief Constable said. 'It was your man Wilson. He wants room made available for someone you've been looking for.'

'Bert Orchard?' Crow asked quickly.

'The same. Apparently he was picked up in Dewsbury a few hours ago and Wilson's bringing him in–' he consulted his watch – 'in about twenty minutes. You'll want to question him here, no doubt.'

'Yes sir, as soon as possible. The other matter–'

The Chief Constable smiled. 'I'll get it under way. A couple of calls, first of all; the locals might have seen Shuffler in their areas and that could narrow the search. I just hope it won't be as long a haul as the last time. As soon as we get word I'll send a car out.'

'I'm grateful for your assistance.'

The Chief Constable's mouth expressed its appreciation of the sentiment. 'It's only right we should work together – you're helping us out, after all. Don't like murder cases in my patch – we've plenty of other stuff to handle. Anyway–'

'One other thing,' Crow said quickly. 'I'd like Mrs Orchard brought in as well.'

'The thought had already occurred to me,' the Chief Constable said, reaching for the telephone. 'Goose and gander, that's the way of it, hey?'

Cuckolder and cuckold, thought Crow.

Chapter 7

1

Wilson's broad face showed signs of tiredness, but his eyes were gleaming with suppressed excitement as though he were at last seeing light at the end of the tunnel. Crow had recognized such excitement in him before and knew that Wilson was not easily so moved.

'What was Orchard doing in Dewsbury?' he asked.

'Making his way back, I think,' Wilson replied. 'He's been down in London, but my guess is he felt out of depth there and wanted to contact Doris.'

'Well, he'll make contact today,' Crow said. 'I want to see him first, but then I'll have them both in together. I want to see what happens when they both get probed at once.'

Wilson leaned forward. 'Before you do make a start – and Mrs Orchard is here now, by the way – there are a couple of other things that have come up. It really looks as though the case is boiling up now.'

'Let's have them,' Crow said patiently.

'First, the cipher chap over at York. They tell me he's cracked the shorthand in Rutland's diary and is now making a fair copy for us. It should be here by tomorrow.'

'Good enough. That's the first – what else?'

'Something not quite so clear-cut. Carson's been in touch from the Met. He seems ... well, he's getting rumours but little more.'

'About Earl Robson?'

Wilson frowned, and nodded. 'Yes. Apparently, some journalist connections he's got have been telling him that Robson had something on Conrad Gunther, something he intended exploding in *Scathe*.'

'Robson told me the story died with Rutland.'

'Robson was being less than co-operative,' Wilson said sententiously. 'Even after your visit he intended pressing on with this story about Gunther.'

'What was the story?'

Wilson shrugged helplessly. 'That's the thing. Carson's not been able to find out. His contacts tell him there *was* a story, Earl Robson intended running it in a few days' time, but ... suddenly, no one's talking.'

Crow stared at his hands. The knuckles

stood out bonily, skin stretched tightly across lean fingers. Earl Robson's hands had been slim, elegant, well manicured, a confident reflection of the man himself Confidence: Robson had felt enough in control to try to keep back information from Crow and then publish it in *Scathe*. But not now. One thing could over-ride confidence.

Fear.

'Someone's got at Robson,' Crow said harshly.

'It sounds like it. And if the story – whatever it was – could be damaging to this man Conrad Gunther, maybe...'

Conrad Gunther. Was he strong enough and rough enough to frighten a man who made a living out of scandal and sensation? Crow thought back. His own interview with Earl Robson had left him with the impression that Robson had confidence and bearing ... but not necessarily the *guts* to face up to a threat. The early years of *Scathe* perhaps testified to that: they'd trodden carefully and thrown mud only at people who couldn't fight back.

'Follow it up,' Crow said, unable to keep the anger and disgust out of his voice. 'Ask Carson to keep at it, and drag up anything he can on Robson, his ex-wife, her relationship with Rutland–'

'That's confirmed,' Wilson interrupted. 'They had a fling all right, and Robson didn't like it. But whether he'd go so far as to bash Rutland's head in because of it–'

Wilson's doubtful tone found its echoes in Crow's mind. He couldn't see Robson acting in that way, not personally, at least.

'We'll keep one eye on it,' he said decisively. 'We've got the diary coming from York and that might give us what we need. We've got a man called Shuffler, somewhere on the moors – and we've got Bert and Doris Orchard.'

He marched towards the door and Wilson followed him.

'We'll take the birds in hand first,' Crow said.

Bert Orchard resented being in hand.

He sat slumped in his chair, surly and resentful under Crow's questions. He answered in monosyllables, refusing at first to give any reasons for going to London, denying he had anything to hide, swearing he had no knowledge of Rutland's death when he left the Three Bells, but as time wore on the belligerence in his manner lessened. His voice weakened under the steady cold persistence of Crow's questions, and Crow began to see his toughness as nothing more than a skin, generated as a defence to guilt and terror. Like a skin it was being shredded away, and Bert Orchard's face became greyer as he sat there, pinned by the questions.

Yet his answers did not change. His eyes became flat and dull, his face swung loosely as he shook his head in denial, but the denials continued.

Crow turned to Wilson. 'All right.' he said in a cold voice. 'Let's have the woman in.'

She came in carefully, as though fearing that to recognize Bert'd be to involve her as an accessory to something heinous, but Bert struggled to his feet in a surprising gesture of gallantry – surprising, until Crow realized just how much Bert Orchard felt he needed the woman. Her, and her testimony. He lurched as he stood there, as though drunk.

Drunk on fear, Crow thought. It gave him the clue to his approach.

Doris Orchard was still keeping her head up. She was not yet prepared to tell the whole truth. She had given Crow as much as she intended giving and, as he took her through her previous statements, she was unmoved. But something was happening to Bert Orchard, nevertheless. He seemed to shrivel under her words as though he found humiliation in them. Carefully, Crow went over it all again.

'Now let's get this clear. For a period of six weeks or so Charles Rutland used to drink at your pub occasionally, and later visit you upstairs. And Mr Orchard knew about this.'

'He didn't care,' she said firmly, and Bert moved slightly on his chair.

'He didn't care, he wasn't concerned about the fact that you were upstairs having intercourse with another man. I find that hard to believe,' Crow said in a mild tone.

'We had our arrangement.'

'And the night in question was like any other?'

'More or less,' she said indifferently.

'But not *quite* the same, surely. You did say Rutland was different. How did his *difference* affect you?'

A nervous hand stole up to pat ineffectually at the beehive blonde hair. 'I don't know what you mean.'

'Did it make you upset, angry, annoyed? Did it cause you to complain to Bert Orchard? Did it make you needle him?'

'It didn't affect me in any way, I told you.'

Crow leaned forward like a great black bird with a hairless skull, a vulture reaching for its prey. 'Then let me tell you something. When Bert Orchard was picked up in Dewsbury we gave him a medical inspection. I have the report in front of me. The doctor states his hands and knuckles are bruised, the skin torn as though he'd been fighting. Someone at the Three Bells? Did he throw out a drunk? Or did he batter Charlie Rutland with his fists? Batter him, then pick up the poker to beat him to death?'

Orchard tried to get up in protest. 'I–'

'Shut up!' Doris turned on him, snarling the word, but something had happened to her face. Crow saw the scoring of indecision around her eyes, and pressed on.

'I can piece it together, more or less,' he said sharply. 'Bert Orchard cared all right but didn't want to lose you. This way, he kept you. Rutland came to you a number of times but you were never his kind of woman – he was slumming, you were an interlude, and that night he used you in a way you didn't like, showed you what he really thought about you. When Bert came upstairs you told him about it, you reviled Rutland to him, urged Bert to behave like a man and teach Rutland a lesson for treating you like a whore. Was that the way of it? Or were you both dissatisfied with the money he paid?

Maybe you sent Bert around just to scare Rutland – he wasn't a very big man. But Bert went too far, didn't he? Makes no difference, you know, Mrs Orchard, no difference at all. If you did send Bert around there, for whatever reason, you're an accessory to–'

Bert Orchard almost howled, like a dog in agony. 'I tell you I didn't–'

Again Doris rounded on him with an expletive that silenced him immediately. Her blonde hair was beginning to fall out of control, and she sat heavy-eyed, staring at Bert, weighing up five years past with him against the possibility of unspecified years ahead in prison. She reached her decision quickly and positively. 'I didn't send him; it wasn't my idea!'

'*You bitch.*'

Crow ignored the man but saw the woman shiver.

She wasn't cold but the shiver continued. Doris had taken a step that frightened her. Crow could not be sure it was a step towards the truth or a leaving behind of the security of the past.

'Better tell me exactly what happened.'

'It's mainly as I said before. Charlie came to me, he acted as though he was wound up tight and I was a whore, he left me and I was shaken. But then Bert came up and ... and *he* wanted me too. I told him to go to hell. He tried anyway so I told him the truth. He was no good.'

The room was silent suddenly and Bert Orchard sat as though carved in stone. Hurriedly, ashen-faced, Doris went on. 'Afterwards he was mad as hell. I tried to stop him but he dressed and went out. He said he was ... he went after Charlie. When he came back, about an hour later, there was blood on his clothes. He burned the trousers in the field back of the pub next day, after we heard Charlie had coughed it. Bert said he'd better go down to London a while.' She shot a quick, malevolent glance at the man beside her. 'I guess he didn't have the guts or the sense to stay down there.'

Crow waited but she said no more. Carefully, he asked, 'What did Bert say before he left the Three Bells to look for Rutland?'

It was as though the man was not in the room with them, as though they were talking of an absent stranger. But Doris was still shivering slightly.

'He said ... he said he'd kill him.'

'You bitch.'

There was no force behind Bert Orchard's words.

This time they came out flatly, a statement of undeniable fact. Doris had refused to support his story, was running out on him, saving herself by pushing him in deep. But there was no more violence in him; he had lost the capacity to react.

'Do you have anything to add to what she's said?' Crow asked him, but Bert stared at him dully. Crow repeated the question and Bert said, 'I didn't kill him. I bashed him, yes. I did that, but I don't know nothin' about any poker. That bitch, she told me I was the only chap who ever turned her on and then, that night...'

He grimaced suddenly, writhing his lips back over his teeth in a gesture of anger. 'But I didn't kill him. I left him in the hall. I swear...'

Crow looked at Wilson and nodded. Wilson stood up, touched Orchard's elbow and led him from the room. There would be more questions now, and finally a statement. It could be the end of the case, but Crow had never been a man to see things so clearly and positively. He watched Doris Orchard's heavy face for a moment and then, almost conversationally, he asked, 'Do you think Bert killed him?'

A faint surprise touched her face, but was

shaded out by indifference as though she had already written the man out of her life. Perhaps she had.

'I don't know. He says he didn't.'

'Is he capable of murder?'

She was looking into the past, looking for the face of a murderer sharing her bed for five years. She wasn't successful.

'Accidental, yes, he could have killed him in a fight. But he said Charlie didn't fight. And I can't see Bert with a poker in his fist. He used to be a boxer, you know. He ... he's still got the legs.'

She put her hand on the chair he had used and it was almost a gesture of possession. She seemed about to cry.

'There are a couple of other matters I want to discuss with you.'

'I don't know a thing more than I told you.'

'It's something you've already told me. Rutland's attitude when he came to you that night. You said he seemed nervy, excited, almost triumphant about something. And he attacked you.'

'Pushed me, I said. I had a go at him then – but he hardly seemed to be aware of me hitting him.' It afforded her a certain resentment, even now. 'It was as though he was thinking about something else.'

'You told me he was laughing, and saying something,' Crow reminded her. She shrugged, folded her hands one inside the other in her lap and stared at the floor.

'He was talking about money. Bleedin' money, he kept saying, bleedin' money.' She frowned suddenly and looked up at Crow. 'No, it wasn't that. *Bloody* money, he said, bloody money, bloody money.' Her puzzlement began to spread over her face, touched her mouth, turned down its ends like the sad fingers of age. 'No, it wasn't that either. Not bloody money. Blood. Blood money. Aw hell, I don't know ... something like that anyway.'

'You don't know what he meant?' She shook her head.

'What'll happen to Bert?'

'He'll be questioned. He'll make a statement. Then ... we'll see.' Crow picked up a pencil and began to play with it. 'You know Rutland wandered around the country quite a bit – driven in a hire-car. Did he ever talk about it?'

'No.'

He questioned her for several minutes on the theme, but it became apparent Rutland had not confided in her. At last Crow turned to another matter. 'One other thing – a foreigner stayed at the Three Bells a

120

couple of months back. You can't have seen many foreigners there – do you remember him?'

She puckered her brow.

'I think so. He stayed just one night, or maybe it was two. Didn't like the look of him. The police asked about him later. Wasn't much to tell.'

'Can you remember his name?'

She shrugged. 'Foreign name. Something Russian. Like Popoff. No, that's stupid, not Popoff. Romoff ... something like that ... Romanoff, that was it, Romanoff.'

'You don't know where he went from the Three Bells?'

She shook her head.

'And he was alone?'

'Quite alone.'

She had been about to say more, but she stopped suddenly and the frown returned to her face, but more deeply, more intense.

'He was there by himself,' she said wonderingly, 'but I remember now, he met someone in the bar, he was talking to a chap in the bar and they were laughing, laughing fit to bust.'

'Was it someone he knew before? Someone local?'

She shook her head quickly and excitedly. 'No. They sort of shook hands as though they hadn't met before but they were laughing as they did it. And ... my God!' She glared at Crow in excited suspicion. 'How did you know about that?'

Something flickered deep in Crow's chest. He dropped the pencil on the desk and leaned forward. 'What do you mean?' he asked.

Suspicion stained her face. 'I remember it now. That foreigner – the time he stayed at the Three Bells. It was the first time I clapped eyes on Charlie Rutland, first time he looked me over too.'

'And the man Romanoff was talking to in the bar?'

'That's who it was,' she said, snapping out the words in the triumph of recall. 'It was Charlie Rutland!'

2

The evening sun dipped behind Bleak Hey, sending red-gold fingers down into the dales below, and the wind rose, picking its way up over the hill, soughing through the tough moorland grass like a stealthy lover hurrying to an assignation.

The brook was hidden from sight, but its

soft chuckling came up on the breeze, and the trees in the little valley moved softly, bending their topmost branches as though in benediction as Shuffler went scurrying past, over the broken crags and the heather, down towards the brook and under the shadow of the hill.

He had sat for almost two hours watching them. Against the grey wall of stone, lichen-encrusted crag, he had sat bracing his back with the dead hare at his feet, limp, long-eared, pathetic. He had seen the car nose its way up the dale, sunlight flashing from its shiny black bodywork; he saw it reach the gate and the track, and the uniformed men had got out. They had stood there for a while, looking up towards Bleak Hey and the shepherd's hut that was Shuffler's refuge, and then they had started the long climb in the late afternoon sunshine, through warm grass cropped close by wandering sheep. Shuffler had sat still, watching them climb, and the obscenities had rumbled in his throat.

They wouldn't leave him alone, the police, and he hadn't done nothing to them. So let them climb and puff in the afternoon, and search for him at the hut; he would sit and wait for them to go away.

But they didn't go away. His anger and

resentment grew as the hare stiffened at his feet and the sun began to dip. The car sat quietly down in the dale and the police were at the hut. They saw the signs that he had been using it and they decided to wait. So, at last, Shuffler decided to stop waiting.

He tied the hare to the cord at his waist, tightened the belt so that it held in the billowing black coat that he wore over ancient trousers and grey woollen shirt thick and stiff with dirt and dried sweat, and left the hill. He followed the line of the heather and the gorse; he came over the shoulder of the hill and made his way down towards the far side of the dale. He passed the last broken crags, headed for the cover of the leaning, wind-plucked trees, and reached the brook.

There he paused for a while, thinking, as the evening sun speckled the ground with golden patches among the shadows. He couldn't think what the police wanted with him. His cans hung from his waist, held in stiffly with his elbows to prevent them clanking as he walked, he had his money on him so there was little lost, little left at the hut for the police to steal. But what would they want with him? Perhaps there had been more trouble, theft, burglary in one of the villages. The hell with that: he hadn't been

124

down the hill in weeks. Hadn't even seen anyone, except the feller who'd given him the money. The money in the can.

He touched it with his grimy fingers, and looked about him. The hollow down at the stream, under the tree. It was as good a place as he knew. He hurried across the darkening grass and found the tree leaning over the brook; he thrust his hand into the cavity at its roots, drew out animal rubbish and smelled field mice, untied the can from his waist, and thrust it deep into the cavity. He scratched his whiskery face, and the smell of the field mice excrement became part of the odours that clung to his cheeks under the encrusted beard.

He packed leaves and branches into the cavity, stood up and away from it, gazed about him suspiciously, and then hurried across the brook to the path at its far side and began to make his way down the dale.

If the police were looking for him, maybe they'd do like last time and follow all his old tracks, visit each of his haunts. But he could fool them: there was a new place this spring, not three miles from here, at Spadger's Farm, and he'd be out of their way there.

Coppers was bastards.

Shuffler trotted on his way down through

the dale and he was happier; the cans began to clank as he went, and it was a merry sound, a free, happy sound. Until he rounded the bend in the stream and saw the bridge carrying the road and the man on the bridge. The clanking stopped abruptly as he stilled it with a nervous hand and stared at the man staring at him.

He was dressed in a dark suit, and he was leaning casually on his elbows on the old stone of the bridge. He was watching Shuffler with an air of indifference, and his bald head seemed to glow under the last tints of sunset. He had deep-set eyes and bushy eyebrows and he looked tall. And skinny. Skinny as hell.

Shuffler didn't know him; didn't want to know him.

Shuffler put his head down and jog-trotted forward, reached the bridge and began to climb up the bank. To his consternation the stranger on the bridge strolled casually across towards him as he climbed, and Shuffler was aware of his height and his jutting, prominent nose. Shuffler tried to hurry the last few feet, scrambling up to the road, grabbing at the grass tussocks with lean fingers hardened by grubbing for a living, but the stranger's stride lengthened and he reached the end of the bridge just as Shuffler did.

Shuffler was breathing fast and angrily as the tall man stood there, almost barring his way. He touched the cans at his waist and was glad he'd hidden the money can.

'You're Shuffler,' the tall man said quietly. A bastard copper.

Shuffler looked along the road and swore under his breath. A car was parked under the hedge fifty yards away, out of sight of the brook. There was a man standing beside it; even now, he was beginning to walk forward, quickly.

'My name is Crow,' the tall man said as Shuffler hesitated, poised for a quick scramble back down to the brook. The words plucked the initiative from Shuffler like the string from an orange: the name and the man's appearance gave him cause for wonder, and he stared at the ungainliness, the boniness, the death's head, and he overcame his initial panic.

'You're a bastard copper,' he said in a surly growl.

'That's right,' Crow said mildly. 'And I want to talk to you for a while.'

'I don't talk to bastard coppers.'

'But you'll talk to me.'

The confidence in Crow's tone made its

mark upon Shuffler. He didn't like coppers, he didn't like their looks, he didn't like their way of life. He didn't like that bastard copper coming up from the car, seen his likes all over Yorkshire, hard, tough and prepared to put the boot into you when you huddled out of the wind in a shop doorway in the Headrow. No, he didn't like coppers but he respected strength. Not force, he could take his thumps as good as the next man, but strength was different. You could feel strength in a man like you could in a hillside or in a stream or in a great lonely crag on the moor. This copper had that sort of feel: the confidence and strength of existence, just existence, like the hill and the stone. Shuffler knew about that.

But this was a bastard copper and he didn't talk to bastard coppers. Shuffler squinted sourly at Crow. 'You sent them up to Bleak Hey after me?'

Crow nodded. 'Yes. I'll call them down now I've found you. I watched the hill, calculated you might come down through the dale.'

'You bastard.'

'I want to talk to you, Shuffler.'

The other man had now joined them. Shuffler saw him wrinkle his nose as he came within wind, and Shuffler showed him his stained broken fangs under his whiskers.

'I won't talk if *he's* here. Bastard copper.'

Crow didn't look around. 'Wait at the car, Wilson. Shuffler and I will talk.'

Reluctantly, Wilson turned and walked back to the car. Shuffler watched him go and then turned to Crow. 'I got to go. I got a place.'

'A few questions first.'

'I don't talk to–'

'A man came to see you recently.'

Shuffler was silent. He peered cunningly at Crow and twitched his whiskers like a rabbit, but he was thinking about animal smells and a cavity and a can of money. He chewed his lip with a brown dogtooth and considered. He touched the empty cans at his waist for reassurance and they clanked.

'What sort of man?'

'You tell me,' Crow said.

Strength and confidence and you had to live in this world, use the heather and the sky, and a cell was good only when the snow and the rain ached your bone into pain. So Shuffler told him about the man but not about the money. He told him all about the man so he wouldn't have to tell him about the money. Bastard coppers didn't need to know about money: he'd earned it, hadn't he? So he described the man, told Crow about how he was short with curly hair and thick lips, well dressed, eager for information.

'What sort of information?'

Shuffler shrugged and the cans clanked. 'He was just askin' around. Said he'd heard I knew the dales and the moors. Asked me about hidin' places and lonely spots. Wanted to know whether I'd seen somethin' funny gain' on up at Menstone or Bleak Hey or wherever.'

'And had you?'

'I walk the hills night-times,' Shuffler said in a surly tone. 'I see lots of things. That's what I told him.'

'He's dead, you know that?'

Everything died. But Shuffler knew what this copper meant and he didn't like that kind of death. He was suddenly nervous and he wanted his hands on that can with the money. He half turned as though to scramble down the bank again, but the bastard copper grabbed him by the arm and his fingers were like steel pins, hard and strong as hell, and Shuffler froze as they bit into his arm.

'His name was Rutland and someone bashed his head in with a poker. The nights can be long up here, Shuffler, and if you went that way who'd there be to hear you call out?'

'There wasn't much I could tell him,' Shuffler said with a sudden gasp. 'There was only Lockyer's Tarn, that's all I could say. Lights up there one night and I took a look, but that's all. He didn't ask no more, was all he wanted, and he went away then. Didn't see him again. You're hurting my arm.'

The fingers did not relax. The eyes were hooded and dark under the heavy brows as Crow frowned at him. 'What about Lockyer's Tarn?'

'Nothin' more than that. I seed lights there, I took a look and I saw the car and then I went on. But next morning when I came back it wasn't there. That's all.'

'Do you know much about cars, Shuffler? Can you recognize the make of a car?'

Shuffler grunted his displeasure. He shook his head. 'He asked me that. I couldn't tell him. Except it was ... didn't look like an English car.'

'A Volvo?' Crow asked softly.

'How the hell do I know? All I can say is there was a car up there, at Lockyer's Tarn.'

'Did Rutland ask you if it was a Volvo?'

'He may've done, I don't remember if he did, you're hurtin' my bloody arm!'

The fingers relaxed their fierce grip, but kept hold of Shuffler's skinny arm.

'Was there anything else?' Shuffler shook his head.

'How did Rutland come to seek you out in the first place?'

'Someone told him I walked the hills and was up around Lockyer's Tarn that partickler night.'

'And that's all you could tell him?'

'About the car,' Shuffler said, and tugged his arm free angrily. 'That's all there was.'

'Nothing else?'

'Nuthin'.'

No word about the money, Shuffler thought savagely as he made his way back up the dale to the hidden can and his shepherd's ruin above Bleak Hey, no word about the money and the way Rutland had laughed, and no word about the other man either, and Lockyer's Tarn. Rutland had paid for that information; coppers didn't pay.

Besides, you didn't tell coppers no more'n you was forced to. All coppers is bastards and always was.

3

The police motor-cyclist arrived at Joe Bembridge's hotel at eight next morning, and

Wilson came out from the breakfast-table to collect the package he brought. He took it into the dining-room where Crow was still munching toast, and he handed it to Crow without a word. Crow finished his toast and poured another cup of coffee before opening the package. It contained Charles Rutland's diary and several sheets of typescript. Crow scowled.

'The expert at York has deciphered the diary. Here, you read it. I hate having a good breakfast spoiled.'

Crow sipped his coffee and watched Wilson as the Yorkshireman eagerly read the typescript. He watched the eagerness change to frustration, saw the beginnings of a frown appear on the broad face, and noted the way Wilson's mouth turned down at the corners. Disappointment and puzzlement; but finally they were replaced by surprise and a renewed interest.

'Wilhelm Grunfeld,' he said.

'Never heard of him.'

'Neither have I, sir. But his name appears in Rutland's diary – several times.'

Crow raised his eyebrows. 'So?'

'So the York office has been researching him for us, as a result of the entries. They thought the information might be useful, though it all seems a bit ancient history to me. Still, it's here...'

'So tell me,' Crow said, and sipped his coffee. Wilson looked back over the notes in his hand.

'Wilhelm Grunfeld was a Gestapo officer in France during the German occupation. He was born in Aachen in 1915... He achieved early prominence in the Hitler Youth Movement and was a Leader in 1936. By 1941 he had become a member of the Gestapo and was based for a while in Paris and Dieppe. During his stay in Dieppe he played a part in uncovering the Sigmund Conspiracy, for which he was decorated by the Fuhrer himself. He was also responsible for the arrest of the Latour group–'

'The French Resistance group in Dieppe?' Crow asked quickly. Wilson nodded.

'It seems that Herr Grunfeld personally headed the arrests and brought the group back to Paris.'

Crow pushed his coffee-cup away from him and touched the table napkin to his thin lips. His eyes were suddenly hard.

'The name Grunfeld is beginning to ring bells,' he said. 'As I remember it, Latour and all his group – six of them, wasn't it? – were murdered.'

'That's what it says in the papers here.' Wilson replied. 'They were taken to Gestapo headquarters in Paris, Grunfeld interrogated them, and they were never heard of after that. It would seem that they were all killed by Grunfeld's order.'

Carefully, Crow folded his table napkin and placed in down on the tablecloth. The war was such a long time ago, and yet it could still raise strong emotions in him. He suddenly felt that this room was full of those old times, as though the people and events were still here in the hotel, breathing, living, occurring. He pushed the thoughts aside as Wilson went on.

'Grunfeld was recalled to Berlin early in 1944. He was involved in the defence of the city, and there was a report that in 1945 he fell into the hands of the US forces. It would seem they didn't hold him for longer than a couple of days, however. He managed to escape and simply disappeared. He's never been discovered since. He was tried in 1949, *in absentia,* in a French court, and found guilty of the murder of Latour and his group. He was sentenced to death. If the French ever do get their hands on him, he'll be executed. They have long memories.'

'It's over twenty years ago, almost thirty.'

Crow mused. 'But why should Charles Rutland be interested in the career of Wilhelm Grunfeld?'

Wilson shook his head, and turned over the sheets of typescript.

'There are a couple of queries here about Grunfeld, noted in Rutland's diary at the time he was in West Berlin. I can only assume he picked up some information which was perhaps leading him to Grunfeld. Though why it should send him running back to Yorkshire thereafter...'

'Is there any other reference to Grunfeld among the papers?' Crow asked, and waited while Wilson quickly read through the loose sheets.

'The only thing I can see – apart from the general query, which the York office has answered for us with this dossier, anyway – is a short list, headed with Grunfeld's name. It's a check list: it begins ... well, look for yourself.'

Crow took the sheet and read it.

Wilhelm Grunfeld. Check:
(a) Date of birth – January 15, 1915
(b) facial characteristics
(c) number and sex and names of children
(d) signature correspondence

Crow frowned.

'Signature correspondence?– What's he mean by that?'

'I've no idea. But that's all there is, as far as I can see. The Berlin trips are largely noted as expenses checks apart from that note. I'll go through them carefully now, of course, but–'

'Go through them *very* carefully, Wilson. And keep your eyes open for the name Romanoff.'

'The stranger who stayed at the Three Bells?'

'And who was met by Charles Rutland,' Crow said. 'You know, things are beginning to move, it seems to me. We can't see the pattern yet, but the pieces are all there – I've the feeling they'll all fit into place for us pretty soon. Charles Rutland, flying between Berlin and Yorkshire; a stranger called Romanoff in the Three Bells; notes on Wilhelm Grunfeld and a story on Conrad Gunther, which might, to say the least, be embarrassing for that "honest soldier of the Third Reich"; a search around the countryside for a tramp called Shuffler and lights on the moor at Lockyer's Tarn–'

'And there's the Orchards too, sir,' Wilson

added quietly.

'Peripheral only, I suspect,' Crow said. 'I'm beginning to feel that Bert Orchard is telling the truth. Maybe he did go around there and knock Rutland about, but that's where it ended. Somebody else finished Rutland off. So Orchard's part is peripheral, I believe. But Doris Orchard ... you remember what she said about Rutland's attitude? About his excitement, what he said before he made love to her, when they were fighting?'

'Blood money,' Wilson said.

'And what does that mean? How would you define the term?'

Wilson screwed up his eyes in thought, like a little boy trying to remember his sums. 'Blood money ... I suppose it's any money you'd get by laying or supporting a capital charge against someone – at least, that was the old idea. I mean, it's payment for informing, isn't it?'

Crow nodded and smiled. 'The danger was, of course, that the charges laid might not be true. False charges – but you'd still get your money if the accused person was hanged.'

'I don't really see the relevance–'

'Nor do I, not yet, not entirely. But perhaps it's a mistake to take Rutland's words too literally. Let's keep them in mind, nevertheless: perhaps the charges he had in mind were false, perhaps they weren't. Either way, I suspect from what Doris Orchard's told us, he was after blood money all right – so someone killed him rather than pay it.'

'You mean Rutland was a blackmailer?'

'It's beginning to look that way. *Scathe* magazine was certainly the kind of rag that would give him a good training for that kind of operation.'

'So where do we go from here?'

Crow rose abruptly and headed for the door. 'I want you to follow up those papers. Carry out a complete check on Wilhelm Grunfeld and do the same thing for Conrad Gunther. I have a sneaking suspicion that maybe Gunther wasn't above providing a place for an ex-Nazi in his business operations. We may find that friend Rutland discovered Gunther knew about Grunfeld – and Rutland thought he could embarrass someone into paying him blood money. Or maybe it's all a red herring. Find out.'

'If I come up with anything, where can I contact you?' Wilson asked as he followed Crow out through the door.

'I'm following the other line. You've got those papers – chase them up. Me, I'm going out to try to discover just why Charlie Rutland was so interested in Shuffler and Lockyer's Tarn.'

'Any ideas about what you'll find there?'

'One idea. And it may well be just what we're looking for to crack this case right down the middle.'

Chapter 8

1

Grey stone walls webbed the dales below them like a spider's tracery, and the cottages nestling under the slopes were like tiny doll houses in the distance. To the east the moors rose higher, reaching up to misty hills where a line of bedraggled trees covered the skyline with dark green, like the drape of a tattered green shawl.

Ahead of Crow lay Lockyer's Tarn, wide and deep, set in a harsh bowl that seemed to have been gouged out of the hillside by a giant hand. At the far side of the tarn blue smoke stained the sky, bracken and wood burned by a crofter clearing the ground, but here the tarn lay forbidding, its waters silver-black and rippled, its edges stony, sedge littering the shallows and high rocks shadowing the deeper water under the hill.

Crow had walked around the tarn. With two senior officers of the local police he had inspected the shoreline but had found nothing of significance. The tarn was a mile and a half in circumference, and there was no telling where anything might have entered the water, if the assumption that something *had* entered it was accurate.

It would not have received many visitors, this tarn.

It was a gloomy place set in a landscape that was harsh and unattractive. Down in the dales there was rolling green land dotted with sheep, but up here everything seemed as dead as the silver-black water.

'It'll be expensive, dragging this place,' one of the officers remarked doubtfully. Crow agreed.

'What about a helicopter?' he asked.

'Catterick could supply one fast enough, but what–'

Crow explained. A helicopter, sweeping above the lake, might see dark shadows in the depth of the tarn that would be invisible to anyone standing on the shore. So rather than start a sweep of the whole tarn with frogmen and dragging equipment, it was decided to call in the Army.

The morning wore on. Just before lunch Crow heard the chatter of rotor-blades and saw the helicopter coming in above the moor. He and the other officers watched it as it started its first sweep, then an Army major arrived in a jeep, together with air-to-ground equipment. He was young and full of enthusiasm; it was an enthusiasm Crow could not share. He always felt there was something grubby about these operations, and excitement never touched him when anything was found, for inevitably a find meant death – of a woman, a child, a man.

There was no excitement in it for him, only sadness.

He watched the sweeps of the helicopter for an hour or so, and the Army major came out of the jeep to chat to him. The conversation was notable only for its inanity. He was a very young major.

At two o'clock the helicopter seemed to have completed its sweeps, but the major explained that the shadows of the crag above the tarn had made spotting difficult in the deepest part of the tarn. Within the hour the sun would have moved sufficiently in the sky to allow a better sighting to be made. The helicopter chattered away and came to rest on the brow of a distant hill, the major roared off in his jeep to get some lunch and one of the officers returned with sandwiches and a flask of tea.

Crow ate his sandwiches apart from the

others, standing on the crag, looking down into the waters of the tarn. The quietness of the place depressed him; the darkness of the place touched him coldly. A car had come up here, Shuffler had seen its lights and perhaps more, and Rutland had made enquiries of Shuffler. Then he died. The key to his death could well lie under these cold waters.

At three o'clock the helicopter lifted off the hill and came chattering back down towards the tarn. It came with a steady deliberation this time, heading for the crag as though it knew exactly what it was looking for, knew exactly where to look. The machine banked, hovered and then dropped lower towards the surface of the tarn until finally the down-thrust of air from the rotors churned the water into a maelstrom. Then it rose again, hovering high like a malevolent bird, and Crow stared at it, almost hating it, for he knew what it meant, this hovering.

The jeep roared into life and came careering and bouncing over the tussocky grass. The major emerged and waved to Crow.

'There's something down there!' he shouted excitedly.

Crow had always thought there would be; if not there, somewhere in the tarn. Some-thing big, at the bottom of the tarn; big and dark, like a car.

A Volvo.

He left the arrangements for the drag to the local men. They would send up lifting equipment, lorries, a crane, once the frogmen had gone down and made their first inspection. There was no need for Crow to stay. He left Jones, the liaison officer, to keep a watching brief for him, and he himself took a car back to Leeds, leaving a message for Wilson at the hotel. He caught the London train and was met at King's Cross by a police car. In the early evening he spoke at length with Carson from the Metropolitan Division and then he went home.

Martha was surprised to see him. Her surprise was overlaid with considerable pleasure. That was one thing he liked about Martha: after so many years of marriage he could still feel the warmth in his chest when she gave him a hug. Other people might see them as oddly assorted: Martha short and getting heavy now, Crow tall, almost skeletal in build. It had never bothered them, the picture they presented. They knew what they had.

Next morning John Crow went to pay his second visit to Earl Robson at the *Scathe* magazine office.

Earl Robson still expressed commitment to his good looks. His suiting was carefully chosen, his tie and shirt were right. His hair was as carefully groomed as his expression. But his eyes were wary, and in the pale sunlight of the cloudy morning his skin seemed waxy and artificial, synthetic as his smile of welcome.

'I wasn't expecting you, Inspector Crow.'

'I had hoped a second visit would not be necessary,' Crow said coldly, 'but it's been forced on me by your lack of co-operation.'

'How can you say that?' Robson spread elegant hands in deprecation. 'This chap Carson from the Metropolitan Division has been around twice, and I've given him all the assistance I could. I gave him everything–'

'But Rutland's files on Conrad Gunther.'

Robson's tone was neutral and guarded. 'I can't give you what I don't possess. Rutland left no files.'

'Carson spoke to your office staff. There were files all right. And I want to see them.'

Robson's eyes flickered; he hesitated, as though he was trying out in his mind several answers, ranging from prosecution to defence. He decided upon the latter.

'I agree there were – are – files belonging

to Rutland. You're welcome to see them. But I checked them myself. They contain no reference to Gunther. That story – if there was indeed a story other than in Rutland's imagination – is now dead.'

Bluntly, Crow said, 'Was it money or threats that made you call off the story? Don't bother to deny it, Robson: we have information that there *was* a story all right, even after I left you here a few days ago, but you killed it. I want to know why.'

'You're making a mistake, Inspector Crow,' Robson said. It was a remark he made several times during the next few minutes and Crow realized that he was getting nowhere. Bought off, or frightened off, it made no difference. The story on Conrad Gunther was dead: *Scathe* would not be publishing an expose on the German businessman, sanctions-breaker or not. Crow changed his tack.

'You told me Rutland made many enemies; you suggested he was an unpleasant man, and I presumed his enemies had been made by his writings in *Scathe*. But was that all of it?'

Robson wrinkled his brow; then remembered what it did to his looks and smoothed the wrinkles away. His face became bland. 'I don't know what you mean.'

'Did he ever use the stuff he dug up about people for his personal profit?'

Robson caught on at once.

'Blackmail? Hell, I don't know. It's possible, but it never came to my attention. I wouldn't want to know of course – he was a bastard with a bitter temper and a macabre sense of humour, but he turned in good stuff for the magazine. What else he did with it was his affair. You've got evidence to suggest–'

'Where were you the night he died, Robson?'

Earl Robson's face became waxier still. He leaned back in his chair slightly as though he had just discovered that Crow was touched with an infection he might transmit. His voice sounded very distant.

'I was at a party in Chelsea. I can produce people who–'

'You could always have arranged it, of course,' Crow said casually. 'Paid someone, I mean, to go up there and batter Rutland to death.'

'I had no reason. He worked for me. I didn't like him, but if I wanted to kill everyone I didn't like–'

Crow smiled thinly. 'But it was more than that. You probably dislike many people, but they didn't all have an affair with your ex-wife.'

This time Robson's silence was long and protracted.

He made no secret of his efforts to retain control of himself, and when he spoke at last there was a clipped finality in his tone that told Crow he had reached a decision.

'All right, you've been looking into my background. So I'll put it straight for you. My wife divorced me and I didn't like it. I'm prepared to admit it – I'd got used to having her around, and I didn't like losing her. For a while, after the divorce, I kept after her, and when I suspected she was having it off with someone I was crazy enough to get her followed. She found out, called the police, we had a hell of a row about it and I promised not to "molest" her, as she put it, in future. And that's all there is to it.'

'Except the man she was seeing was Charles Rutland.'

Robson sneered.

'It was over pretty quickly. He was a stop-gap for her. It blew over. But let's get this clear: I didn't like Rutland being with her, and I disliked him anyway. But that was over months ago, and Rutland and I never even discussed it. Certainly, it could never have been a reason for me to kill him – my quarrel was with Sandra, and even that's water under the bridge. So don't think you can start pinning motives on me – I just wasn't that interested in Rutland.'

On that issue Crow decided to reserve judgment.

2

The weather broke that afternoon and the rain came hissing down out of a bruised sky. The tarn was touched with a mist that almost covered the crags above it, and the water was a slaty colour, scarred and pitted by the driving rain. A heavy truck was parked at the edge of the tarn; the crane mounted on the back of the truck hung over the water at the spot below the crag where the helicopter had pinpointed the object in the depths. Three police cars were stationed a little distance back and, as Crow got out of the squad car and walked towards the truck, one of the senior officers emerged from the nearest car and came towards him.

Crow lowered his head against the driving rain; he wore no hat and the rain was cold against his bare skull.

'Any luck so far?' he asked.

The police officer hunched deeper in his regulation issue raincoat and shook his head gloomily.

'There are two divers down there – been down all morning in spells. It's a car all right–'

'A Volvo?'

'That's right. If you knew... Anyway, a Volvo it is, but it's causing them trouble. It seems as though it pitched from that crag there straight into the tarn and sank to the bottom. Unfortunately, there are some broken boulders down below, and the nose of the Volvo's got wedged between the foot of the crag and a massive boulder, they tell me.'

'You mean it can't be moved?' Crow asked.

'Not *can't* – but moving it will take some time. If they fix the crane tackle to it and heave, they'd probably pull it free, but equally the heave might tear the car apart. You wouldn't want that.'

Crow *didn't* want that. That car was somehow connected with Charles Rutland and Crow wanted the car in one piece, as untouched as possible. The forensic boys would want to go over it – and who could tell what they'd come up with?

As Crow watched, a movement broke the dark surface of the water. A man's head lifted out of the water like a black seal, shiny and smooth. A moment later a second seal-like head broke the surface: the divers were coming up from their stint below. They turned their masked faces towards the shore and headed for the foot of the crag. Crow made his way down through the rain to meet them.

The first man ashore took off his mask. He was a young man, tall, broad-shouldered, and the thickness of his muscular body was exaggerated by his black diver suit. He unslung his aqualung and lowered it to the ground, then wiped a hand across his face.

'Any progress?'

The diver squinted at Crow and his companion through rain that drove against his face, and then shrugged. 'Some. But it's going to be a slow job. It's deep, that car, and it's firmly wedged. The worst thing about it is the water, though – it's mucky down there, black as the pit and we can't see very much. This rain is only making things worse.'

'When do you think you'll be able to winch the car up?' Crow asked.

'No saying, really. I'd hope to break it out by tomorrow, but it's no joke trying to move it. If we could cut it free now...'

He looked at Crow questioningly, but obviously expected little support for the suggestion. He sighed.

'I could do with some hot coffee... We should get the cable hitched around her this afternoon and we'll try easing her out of there; if that don't work we'll have to drag that blasted boulder out of there.'

He turned, waved to the second diver, and they headed for the truck. The driver leaned from his cab with a flask; the first diver took it and walked awkwardly across to the nearest police car and climbed into the back seat. His companion joined him and they poured out some coffee into two mugs. Crow stood beside the car with his back to the wind. Rain dripped down into the collar of his shirt.

'Windows of the car all closed?' he asked.

The diver shook his head.

'No. Front ones are partly wound down.'

'Could you get into the car?'

'No. The passenger door is locked, and the driver's side is wedged against the rock. Couldn't get in.'

'You could have used a key on the passenger side.' The diver sipped his coffee, grimaced at its hotness, looked at Crow and said, 'Yes, sir, we *could* have.'

'Do it, on your next dive. Take a look inside.'

Crow glanced at the police officer beside him. 'You can get some keys brought up?'

'Immediately.'

The diver was staring at his coffee. He did not seem very pleased at Crow's intervention in what he saw as his specialized job, but he could make no comment to the senior man. Reflectively, if reluctantly, he said, 'There's something in there, though.'

Crow leaned forward, peering into the open window of the car.

'What do you mean?'

'There's something in the car. Couldn't make it out – a bundle of some sort, on the floor in the back. Difficult to see down there, you know: muddy and dirty, and even our flashlights can't do us much good.'

'There's nothing in the front seats?'

The diver shook his head and cupped his hands around the coffee mug.

'Not that we can see. There may be documents and so on under the dashboard, but we can't reach–'

'As soon as you get the car open I want you to get that bundle from the back brought up.'

'Well, it won't be for a while, sir. We need to take a break now, and—'

'Get it up as soon as you can. I'm going back to my hotel to change out of these wet things,' Crow said crisply. 'I can be contacted at Backchapel.'

The diver looked down at his wetsuit. He obviously would have liked a change too. Crow went back to the squad car in the hissing rain.

'Let me know as soon as possible,' he said to the police officer accompanying him.

'We'll do that, sir.'

Crow drove off, away from the gloomy tarn.

He had instructed the driver to take the shortest route to Backchapel and the hotel. He was soon lost as the car took several winding lanes down from the moors, but the police driver, a local man, obviously knew the area well. There was little to be seen in the rain; the mist clouds were down in the dales and everything seemed grey and cold. Crow huddled in the back seat of the car and felt miserable as the wetness spread around from the back of his collar to the front of his shirt. It had been stupid, standing out there in the rain at the tarn. If Martha knew, she'd play hell with him.

He stared out of the window, brushed the condensation from the glass to peer out more carefully. The road had widened, and suddenly seemed familiar. He leaned forward.

'Where are we now?'

The driver inclined his head backwards and sideways.

'Not far to go now, sir. Ten minutes and–'

'Aren't we fairly near Selby Grange?'

The driver nodded emphatically.

'That's right, sir. About half a mile ahead there's a turning on the left; it'll take you up to the Grange.' Crow leaned back in his seat. He pursed his thin lips, considering. A phone call would do as well, there was no need to go up to the Grange a second time. Still...

The road to Selby Grange veered to the left a little way ahead of them. On impulse Crow directed the driver to make the turn, and a few minutes later the squad car entered the driveway of Selby Grange.

Aileen Selby received John Crow in the same room in which he had met her previously. She expressed consternation when she saw the wet state he was in.

'Oh, Inspector Crow – do take off that

coat and–'

'Really, Mrs Selby, it's not necessary. I just thought I'd call in briefly as I was passing, and–'

'No,' she said firmly, 'I insist. You'll catch cold standing around like that. Take off your jacket as well, and I'll order tea for us. Is your driver in a similar state?' Crow smiled. 'He had the good sense to stay in the car. And I won't take off my jacket, Mrs Selby, though I won't say no to a cup of tea. I shan't stop long.'

'Well, as you like.' Aileen Selby moved away, rang a handbell in imperious fashion, and, when the young girl appeared, ordered tea for herself and Crow. Mrs Selby caught Crow's glance.

'A nice child ... I suppose you see it as somewhat anachronistic – a young girl "in service".' She laughed. 'One has to pay far more than used to be necessary, but with work in factories and offices ... still, it's yet possible to get maids. Some of the hill far- mers, their daughters are prepared to follow a tradition...'

She sat down, fixed her green glance on Crow, and smiled. It was a precise, controlled smile; that of a woman who knew what she wanted, knew where she was going. It brought to his mind Joe Bembridge's comment, when they had spoken of Mrs Selby. Aileen Selby was a very capable woman.

'But you won't be here to discuss the servant problem, Chief Inspector Crow,' she said softly.

'Hardly that.' Crow took the seat she waved to, and leaned forward, conscious of his damp collar. 'I really *was* just passing, on my way back to my hotel. But I thought I'd come in and tell you – I think we've found your Volvo.'

Her eyes came more alive, flickers in the green, half-seen, incalculable.

'You've found it? Where – in what condition is it? Really, I–'

'I doubt if you'll be able to use it again,' Crow said. 'If I'm right, it's been lying at the bottom of Lockyer's Tarn for some time.'

'Lockyer's Tarn?'

Mrs Selby frowned fiercely and a spasm of anger crossed her face. It surprised Crow: he had thought her a woman who would have controlled such emotions far better – or at least, controlled the external registration of such feelings.

'How did you find it?' she asked. 'I mean … at the bottom of the *tarn!*'

'It's a long story … but Charles Rutland

must be involved in it. He was looking for that car, I suspect, Mrs Selby. He spoke to an itinerant known as Shuffler, and heard from him that there'd been lights and a car at the tarn – and Shuffler told us the same thing.'

Conflicting emotions chased across her face like shadows over a sunlit hill. Puzzlement, incredulity, and other emotions he could not place. Perhaps anger, that the car her prospective son-in-law had bought her should have been consigned to such a fate.

'But why on earth should this man Rutland ... I mean, what was his interest in my car?'

Gently, Crow said, 'Perhaps we won't know that until we lift it from the tarn.'

She stared at him with parted lips; something was happening to her breathing. 'You think you'll manage that?'

'It's difficult. It's stuck, wedged against a rock, but I think we'll manage it eventually.'

'I still can't understand why Rutland wanted to find it. I mean – well, do *you* have any idea why he should go searching for it, and ask questions of this tramp and so on?'

Crow shook his head. 'No...' The maid entered the room and he waited until she had gone. Each time he came here he seemed to end up being served tea. He noted the silver service was out again in his honour. He watched Aileen Selby pour the tea; her hand was rock steady.

'I've no real idea as yet,' he continued when the girl had gone, 'but it may be it wasn't so much the car he was interested in as what it contained.'

She handed him his cup of tea, frowning.

'I don't understand. There was nothing in the car when I left it at the Merrion Centre.'

'The car was stolen,' he replied. 'There's something in the back now. It's probable that it was of importance to Rutland.'

She shook her head. 'Well, I'm afraid I've no suggestions to make. You're sure it's my car?'

'Not yet. But it is a Volvo, and there's no report of another Volvo missing in the Yorkshire area.'

He stirred his tea after putting in a lump of sugar. He was surprised to note that Mrs Selby had spilled some tea into the saucer: the news he brought about her car was possibly more upsetting than she showed. He felt sorry for her suddenly; it was unpleasant, being involved with police enquiries when her daughter was about to get married.

'Is your daughter still with you?'

'No she flew to Crete this morning.' Mrs

Selby smiled rather wistfully. 'We've seen little of her at Selby Grange these last few years. For that matter, I've not spent much time here myself this last month or so. Having the car stolen was annoying and a tremendous nuisance, but I didn't need it, in fact, because I joined Chris – my daughter's fiancé – and his father on the yacht for a while. I only got back to England a few days ago, in fact. Just time to set things in order here, and then I'm off again. Sooner than I expected, in fact.'

The smile faded. Crow raised his eyebrows and Mrs Selby said, 'It's Chris's father. He's living in Crete now – the climate suits him, though he's Scottish through and through. But he's been ill, you know... And three days ago he had another attack. He's very fond of Ingrid,' she added, almost inconsequentially.

She sipped her tea, replaced the cup and suddenly said, 'When you get this car up, I shan't want it. You suggested it would be a write-off, but even if it wasn't I wouldn't want it. Having it stolen ... it sort of makes it unclean, doesn't it? You know what I mean?'

Crow knew.

'When do you expect to raise it?' she asked.

'Tomorrow, I hope. Er ... Mrs Selby, I don't suppose you can help me on this one, but it's a long shot. I know you told me you never met Charles Rutland, but while he was up here, at the Three Bells, he was observed talking to a stranger ... a foreigner. Did you come across him? I can't give you a description, I'm afraid, but his name was Romanoff.'

'*Romanoff?*' Very regal,' she murmured coldly. Her eyes became reflective as though she were searching deep in her mind, not only the recent past but more distant times, and her mouth hardened. 'I can't say I have come across anyone of that name. I've met a number of foreigners of recent months in my journeying – I even met an Australian in the wool business in Bradford a year ago who knew me as a child in Alice Springs! But Romanoff ... the name is not familiar to me. Russian?'

'Your guess is as good as mine.'

Crow felt a tickling at the back of his throat and he took another sip of tea. He hoped he didn't have a cold coming on.

'I think I'd better be on my way and get a hot bath,' he said. 'I don't suppose you'd have found this sort of climate in Alice Springs, Mrs Selby. You've never wanted to go back to Australia?'

She shook her head positively.

'Australia holds no pleasant memories for me. I was glad to leave. I shall never return.'

Crow recalled hearing about something unhappy there, and fearful that he might be reopening old wounds he finished his tea hurriedly. As he put down his cup Mrs Selby asked, 'Do you think this man Romanoff may be the link between my car and Rutland?'

'It's a possibility, but nothing more. I've not established any such link but ... tomorrow may tell.'

He rose to his feet, thanking Mrs Selby for her hospitality. She gave him his coat and he got into it awkwardly, conscious of his height and gaucheness as he towered over her. He turned to walk towards the door but she put one hand on his arm. Her fingers were slim and elegant, her touch light.

'Inspector Crow, you've not met my daughter's fiancé but I expect you've heard about his father.'

'Mr Santer?' Crow nodded. 'Yes, I know he's built up a big business – biscuits, isn't it? And I've heard your future son-in-law will take over from him.'

'*Has* taken over,' she said quietly.

Crow stared at her. 'When did this happen?'

'Two days ago. It became ... necessary. Of

course, Chris has been groomed to take over for a few years now, but Mr Santer didn't intend... The fact of the matter is he's got a weak heart. He's had a couple of attacks during the last year or so – and he had quite a serious one three days ago.'

'I'm sorry to hear that.' Crow hesitated, a little puzzled as to why Mrs Selby was bringing the matter up again.

'I think you should understand,' Mrs Selby said, 'how it's been with Mr Santer. Like me, he has one child. He's devoted all his love and affection to his son, as I have to my daughter. He carved out the business for him, for Chris; I did my best for my own child. There was almost an ... inevitability about it, that Chris and Ingrid should meet, I mean. For Mr Santer and I are so alike – and we both liked what we saw in each other's children. We were delighted when they decided to marry. Now ... the point is he's been very much in favour of Chris's marriage to Ingrid. He hoped to see a grandson – he told me so, several times. Now, I think he will be happy if only he sees Chris and Ingrid married.'

'I trust that he will Mrs Selby.'

Her hand was still on his arm. 'It's because of that – and his last heart attack – that the wedding is to be brought forward. Mr Santer wants the ceremony this week; we can hardly argue, for in his present physical state–'

'This week?' Crow frowned. 'That means you'll have to get out pretty soon.'

She dropped her hand. Her eyes were very green. 'I'd hoped to take the plane tomorrow morning. I've booked the ticket, but now, well, I wondered whether, in view of the fact you've discovered the Volvo in Lockyer's Tarn, you might feel it was necessary for me to–'

'Identify it?' Crow interrupted. He gave her a warm smile. 'The number plates will tell us all we need to know in that direction. I see no reason for you to worry, Mrs Selby, and no reason for you to stay. Your daughter's to be married – you must be there. But just in case anything does come up I'd be grateful if you'd leave us an address, a phone number, where you can be contacted.'

'I can do that quite easily,' she said, and there was relief stamped on her face. 'Thank you, Inspector.'

Crow sneezed as he hurried down to the car and the patient police driver.

He was still sneezing next morning. The hot bath and a hefty meal at the hotel in Back-

165

chapel seemed to have made little difference, and Crow was annoyed. His temper
was not improved when Detective-Sergeant
Jones told him there was no news from the
tarn yet.

'And Bert Orchard is screaming for bail,'
he added.

Crow swore.

'Have we got the complete report from
forensic yet?'

'Yes, sir. Dr Frust sent it in last night. We're
holding Orchard on a charge of assault at the
moment, assault on the policeman who arrested him, but he's getting surly and wants
out.'

'All right, give me the forensic report and
I'll see Orchard again. Have you seen Wilson this morning?' Jones shook his head.

'He went to York yesterday with some
papers that came from Rutland's bungalow.
He said he'd be back today.'

'Good. If he comes in, tell him I want to
see him. Meanwhile, get that file and–'

The phone on his desk shrilled, and Jones
grabbed for it nervously as though he feared
its tone might slash across Crow's nervous
system. He listened for a moment and then
handed the phone to Crow.

'For you, sir.'

It was one of the senior officers from Lockyer's Tarn. 'Did you get the car up yet?' Crow asked.

'Not yet, but we hope it'll be clear by this afternoon. And we haven't been able to get into the car either. The lock burst on impact and the keys are useless.'

'So you've not been able to get at the bundle in the back?' Crow asked in disappointment. The man at the end of the line hesitated.

'Yes and no. We can't get it out, but we managed to get hold of it through the broken window, and sort of drag at it. Thing is, sir, it isn't a bundle after all.' Crow had almost guessed, right from the beginning, but he asked now. The reply was as he expected.

'It's a *body*, sir. We're sure of it; it's a body in the back.'

'I want that body up as quickly as possible,' Crow said, frowning. The police officer hurried to speak again, anxious that Crow should not ring off.

'There's something else – when the divers tried to pull out what they thought was a bundle and realized it was a body they left it where it was. But the jacket had worked free, and they were able to get a hand into the pocket. There was a wallet in there.'

'Identification?' Crow asked quickly.

'Yes, sir.'

'Don't tell me,' Crow said in a grim voice. 'It's the body of a man, and his name is Romanoff.'

There was a short, puzzled silence.

'Well, no, I'm afraid it isn't. There's a plastic-covered card identifying the dead man, but the name's not Romanoff. It's Schulman – Erich Schulman.'

Crow was taken aback; he would have sworn that the mysterious Romanoff would have been the man Rutland had been looking for during his June visit. 'This card,' the officer continued, 'is one issued by an employing company. It's got Schulman's employer named as–

'For my peace of mind let me try once again,' Crow interrupted sardonically. *'Gunther?'*

The silence at the other end of the line illustrated how impressed the man was; it was a small enough victory, Crow thought sourly.

'That's right,' the man said in a subdued voice. 'Conrad Gunther.'

Crow interviewed Bert Orchard half an hour later. He had Dr Frust's forensic report open in front of him, and he read the details of the report again, keeping Orchard waiting, and sweating, in front of him.

'I understand you want to be released on bail,' Crow said sourly.

'You got no right to keep me here,' Bert Orchard replied, and showed his truculence in his heavy face. 'I keep telling you I had nothin' to do with the murder of Rutland–'

'But you *were* there, and you did hit him – I've got the forensic report here in front of me, and we've enough to connect you with Rutland by way of motive, opportunity and physical–'

'But I didn't *kill* him!'

Crow stared impassively at Bert Orchard. The man was perched on the edge of his chair and his hands were gripped tightly together. There was a fine dew of perspiration along his forehead and he was obviously unnerved by Crow. Yet Crow guessed he was telling the truth: it was a story he had stuck to with Wilson, ever since Doris Orchard had admitted that Bert left her and went down to Rutland's bungalow.

'All right, let's go over it again. When you went to the bungalow were the lights on?'

Orchard nodded vigorously.

'The light in the sitting-room was on. I just went up and pressed the doorbell – I was impatient and I pressed it a second time, and then he opened the door to me.'

'What was his reaction when he saw you standing there?'

Orchard twisted his mouth indecisively and shrugged. 'I don't think he really saw me, you understand. He seemed about to say something but ... but I didn't give him time.'

'You hit him.'

'That's right,' Orchard said, and time and death and the circumstances of arrest could not keep the satisfaction out of his tone. 'As soon as he opened the door I planted one on him, and he went back like a squealing pig.'

Crow consulted the forensic report. 'This would have been the blow that broke his nose?'

Orchard hesitated, but the memory of the blows was too pleasant to be denied.

'Yes. I felt it smack open, spread all over his face. He was wearing a kind of flowered shirt and the blood shot straight down over it. I remember that.'

'And then?'

'He fell back, near the door to the lounge. He tried to get up, opened his mouth to shout, but I wasn't having him making a fuss so I took a flying kick at him. Look, I'm telling you all this so you know it's the truth – I'll tell you exactly but it's got nothin' to do with murder–'

'You kicked him,' Crow said coldly, 'and presumably that drove the breath out of his lungs. He was lying there helpless with a broken nose and a cracked rib and...?'

Orchard licked his lips. He was looking decidedly unhappy but he was no longer keeping anything back.

'I don't remember it all in detail, but I kicked him at least once more and I think he went out – fainted maybe. But I was hot and angry – real savage if you must know because of what Doris had said, and I got down on my knee and I ploughed into him with my fist. I don't know how many times ... but there was blood all over my fist and my trousers... After a while I came to myself, and Rutland was lying there, breathing and bubbling, you know, blood in his nose and throat, and I thought I might do for him lying there on his back. So I turned him over, put him face down so the blood would run out and he'd be able to breathe.' Orchard looked up defiantly. 'I never intended him real harm, you got to realize that!'

Crow stared at Orchard in silent amazement. The publican could hammer at

Charlie Rutland in this way and yet deny he meant him harm. He shook his head. 'All right. What happened then?'

'I left. I went back home, ran to where I'd left the car, drove back to the Three Bells, burned my trousers later in the field. Then, next morning, I heard a rumour that Charlie Rutland had been done in, and I panicked. I thought Doris would stand by me, but I was scared, my hand was marked and all that ... so I pushed off to the Smoke, but it was no good down there. I didn't feel I could leave Doris ... and then I read he'd been done in with a poker, and that wasn't me, I swear I just used my fists and–'

'Why did you run?' Crow enquired softly. Orchard's lower jaw dropped and a stupid look came across his face. 'I just said–'

'From the bungalow. Why did you run back to the car?'

Orchard was silent for almost a minute. He seemed puzzled, but not so much by Crow's question as his own reasons for behaving as he had done. He seemed not to have thought about it before, and now he raised the question in his mind he appeared almost sheepish as he reached a conclusion.

'Well, I don't know. I just came out ... and ran.'

'But Rutland couldn't raise an alarm,' Crow said in a mild, reasonable tone. 'Why run? You had nothing to fear.'

Doubt replaced the sheepishness and struggled with truculence. The truculence won.

'I don't know why the hell I ran. Hell, I don't know ... it was ... well, it was as though I felt I was being watched, you know, as though a copper–'

'*Were* you being watched?' When Orchard stared at him, Crow added, 'I mean, did you *see* anyone when you ran to your car?'

Orchard shook his head slowly. 'No. But ... I felt like eyes were on me. Mind, I was keyed up and–'

'Were there any other cars parked nearby?'

'I don't think–' Orchard stopped, thought for a moment and then said, 'I think there was a car parked about a couple of hundred yards away. No one in it, I'm sure, and I can't remember much what it looked like except it was a light colour. But what–'

'Tell me, Orchard,' Crow interrupted. 'About what time was it when you left Rutland?'

Orchard's reply was surly. 'Can tell you exactly. Church clock chimed. Bloody three in the morning.'

Crow placed a hand flat on the report in front of him. The long, bony fingers rested there, spread out, cold and skeletal. 'Dr Frust tells me,' he said softly, 'that Charlie Rutland died at approximately three in the morning.'

Bert Orchard bounced out of his chair in a fury. 'No bloody doctor's going to pin this thing on me.' He shouted in a sudden violence. 'I tell you I didn't have–'

'Sit down and shut up.' Crow said, and the iron in his tone made Orchard stop, subside at once. He stared at Crow, trembling, then quickly sat down.

'It was three in the morning,' Crow said, 'and Rutland came to the door to answer you almost immediately. He was dressed, moreover, he hadn't gone to bed. You left that bungalow, it was almost three – did you leave the door open?'

'I ... I guess so. I just turned him over, left, ran–'

'And Rutland died within minutes. If you didn't use that poker, Orchard, who did? The person Charlie Rutland was waiting for? The person he came to the door expecting to see? The person who arrived there only a few moments after you clobbered Rutland in the doorway?'

Orchard's eyes went round with relief and excitement.

'You mean he was expecting someone? Hell, of course he was! He'd never have opened the door if he'd known it was me! And like you say, he was dressed, he was expecting someone. Why the hell didn't I think–'

'Again,' Crow said. 'Let's go over it all again. Just in case there's something you left out.'

There was nothing more. Under the feeling of euphoria engendered by the excitement, Bert Orchard went over his story and elaborated upon it: no longer was he scared, running from the house. He felt eyes were on him. When he came out he thought he saw a shadowy figure, a man in a dark raincoat at the corner of the street. When he finally reached his car and looked back, he thought he saw a shadow, standing against the doorway of Rutland's bungalow. And as he drove away the lights went out in the bungalow, and he passed the car. He thought its registration held a 'J'.

But Crow discounted most of it. The elaborations were products of Bert Orchard's belief: his imagination would soon become so fevered that he would start to describe the man in the raincoat, endow him with a specific height, definite features. He'd even give the colour of his eyes if Crow persisted long enough. The hook was no longer biting into Orchard's gullet, so he wanted to settle it firmly into someone else's. But the only item Crow was at all prepared to accept was that the lights went out shortly after Orchard accelerated away – and even that was likely to be a figment of Orchard's imagination.

He made Orchard swear out a new statement, and informed him that he would be appearing before the magistrates in the morning on charges of assault and obstructing the police in the execution of their duty. He did not tell Orchard whether he would be opposing bail or not. Crow then spent the next hour with a small group of newspapermen, telling them nothing, explaining patiently he had nothing of significance to report. It was a chore he hated; on this case the Chief Constable had kept the newspapers off his back and for that Crow was thankful. But it was time he did face them. He was glad when it was over.

He had just taken his third decongestant tablet for the nasal catarrh that was building up when Wilson arrived at Headquarters.

'You look as though you've been hard at it,' Crow said.

Wilson looked tired. His eyes were pouched and heavy, and the light stubble on his chin showed he had not shaved this morning. He sat down across the desk from Crow, settling in the chair with a sigh.

'You can say that again. Been up most of the night.'

'Rutland's diary?'

Wilson nodded. 'And a few other papers that fitted in. I went across to York to have a chat with the cipher expert and so get him to translate the papers, and then I spent a busy night making a few calls to Interpol.'

Crow frowned. He reached for the telephone and rang the canteen, asked them to send up a pot of coffee. Then he leaned back in his chair and folded his arms. 'Gunther?'

Again Wilson nodded. 'The whole story on Gunther. I haven't got it yet, though I can make a pretty good guess at it. I spent a long time sweating over Rutland's notes, and then Interpol did the checking of birth dates and Army records for me. They finally came up with what I wanted about five this morning.'

'Gunther...' Crow said, musing. 'His name keeps cropping up, doesn't it.'

'You've got another lead on him?'

177

'I'll tell you about that in a moment. First of all, let's hear what you've got.'

Wilson picked up his briefcase and took out the pocketbook they had found on Rutland, together with some scattered papers and a notebook of his own. He pushed the diary and the papers towards Crow, and opened his own notebook.

'You can look at these for the corroboration, but I've made a summary of the facts as we have them in here. It all starts, really, in 1952. In that year Conrad Gunther married the daughter of a diamond merchant in Buenos Aires. You'll remember that before that time he had returned to Germany for a while and then moved to South America. Well, marrying this woman gave him entry to society in Buenos Aires, and it gave him some capital backing also. He started an export-import business, and in 1953 backed a conservative political party which gained some notoriety. It made his name, and in 1960 he branched out, set up a machine-tools industry in South Africa, using business contacts initially built up by his father-in-law. It proved successful, and he later expanded in a small way back into Europe.'

Wilson flicked over a page and glanced at Crow.

'He'd obviously developed a taste for globe-trotting, because he also visited Rhodesia at this time, and spent some time in Africa. Anyway, the upshot of it all was a business empire of some consequence, taking in units in South Africa, Rhodesia, Holland and South America. And in two days' time he will be in London, to discuss the establishment of a consultancy, and to inject life into discussions over our own machine-tools industry.'

Crow nodded, and scratched his cheek.

'All right,' he said, 'the honest German soldier makes good. Not an uncommon story. Where does it start to bite? Why was Rutland interested? Was it really over the question of possible trading with Rhodesia, as Earl Robson said? After all, if Gunther had interests in Rhodesia–'

'Let's go back to the year 1953,' Wilson interrupted. 'Gunther was married two years, but there were no children. Instead, suddenly, he adopts one. A con. He brings up the boy as his own, and Johann Gunther is now firmly established on the boards of Gunther's companies.'

'So?'

There was a knock on the door and a constable entered, self-consciously carrying a pot of coffee and two cups on a tray. As Wilson took it from him, Wilson said, 'Take another look at Rutland's diary.'

'I presume you mean the section where he raised queries?'

'That's right – on Wilhelm Grunfeld, the Gestapo officer.'

Wilson poured the coffee while Crow checked back. He sipped his with every sign of enjoyment as Crow looked up.

'All right. There's a query here about the number and sex and names of Grunfeld's children.'

Wilson nodded.

'Right. I've checked with Interpol and they gave me details. Grunfeld, surprisingly, had three children. A girl and two boys. The girl and the youngest son were killed in Berlin in 1943. The older boy survived. His name was Johann.'

Wilson said no more for a moment, and the silence grew around them as Crow contemplated the diary. 'Are you saying that Conrad Gunther adopted the son of Wilhelm Grunfeld, and has brought the boy up as his own?'

'I'm saying just that. Johann Grunfeld flew to Buenos Aires in 1953 and was adopted by Gunther. He is now known as Johann Gunther.'

'Curious,' Crow said.

'Very. But there are other curiosities. Look at the other queries raised by Rutland in that diary. We know that honest soldier Gunther was born in 1915. When was Grunfeld born?'

Crow reached for his coffee. 'At a guess,' he said slowly, 'I'd say ... 1915?'

'And you'd be right. Moreover,' Wilson added, 'Gunther lost the little finger of his left hand as a young boy; when Grunfeld was seventeen he also lost the little finger of his left hand in the Austrian Alps – he was involved in a fall, lost his little finger and broke his jaw, left it somewhat lopsided.'

'And Gunther's facial characteristics?' Crow asked. 'He was injured in a car crash in 1955, and maybe his broken nose and jaw were suffered then ... but he *does* have a sort of lopsided charm to his smile.' He sipped his coffee again.

'So they tell me, anyway.'

'There was one other query – photo and signature correspondence.'

Wilson shook his head. 'Nothing on that. Interpol couldn't free a thing on either man. That was sort of funny, really, but it was as though they were suddenly frozen out. No matter – the use of the word "correspondence" tells us all we need to know, anyway.'

Crow stared at the diary and nodded. 'Charles Rutland wondered whether there would be a similarity between photographs and signatures of the two men.'

'More than wondered,' Wilson suggested. 'My guess is that Charles Rutland knew, in the end, that Conrad Gunther and Wilhelm Grunfeld were *one and the same man.*'

Crow continued staring at the papers in front of him, but he was hardly aware of them. His mind was filled with images of the past, a war-torn Berlin, smoke in the sky, death in the air. A Gestapo officer, desperate to escape, knowing that he would be executed if captured, taking the well-greased escape route used by senior Party members to South America. Then, later, with an identity assumed – using a dead man's name, a man killed probably in Europe – he achieved respectability and success. But he looked back to the older time still, for his son still lived. Grunfeld was depicted by the French courts as a monster, but he had father-feelings, and he had risked a great deal to get his only remaining son by his side once again. A great deal ... if not everything.

Crow looked up at Wilson. 'Shuffler. I want that damned tramp Shuffler brought in. He didn't tell us all we wanted and all he knew.'

'I don't understand, sir.'

Crow grimaced.

'They're pulling a car – that missing Volvo – out of Lockyer's Tarn this morning. There's a body in the back. It's the corpse of a man called Erich Schulman. He was employed by Conrad Gunther. What I want to know is ... did Erich Schulman make contact with this man Shuffler? Because if he did, I begin to see the pattern.'

'I'm still not with you,' Wilson said, scratching his stubble. He looked tired.

'We've been assuming that there was something about the car that interested Rutland – but that was a mistake. Rutland was simply looking for *Schulman*. He'd already met Schulman at the Three Bells, where Schulman registered under an assumed name. Rutland went back to Germany, then when he returned he came to Yorkshire, but Schulman had disappeared. So Rutland did a tour in a hired car, until he found Shuffler who told him about lights at Lockyer's Tarn.'

'And then it was Rutland who got the hammer.' Grimly, Crow pushed the papers aside and stood up.

'We know now why he died. We know now what Rutland meant about *blood money*. It's my guess Schulman was the man who gave

Rutland information about the Gunther/ Grunfeld masquerade. The bungalow was rented to hide Schulman up here, in an out-of-the-way spot, while the squeeze was put on Gunther.'

'Instead of which, first Schulman and then Rutland got squeezed.'

'And Earl Robson got frightened off the story. This man Gunther–'

'He's got a lot to lose,' Wilson said. 'His life, maybe.'

'That doesn't excuse taking others. But Shuffler ... maybe Shuffler can be the confirmation we need. So let's get him.'

Chapter 9

1

It was two days later, and on a moor, drowsy under the hot sun, that they finally found Shuffler. He had forsaken his old haunts, but a farmer told the police that he was up in a decayed crofter's cottage on the moor. They were forced to make their way there on foot across peat-hag and through broom and heather above the wavering heat-mist that almost obscured the dales below. A combination of beer and the hot sun had left him dancing, fighting mad, and he met the policemen with a wild hail of badly directed cans and clods of earth and stones. There was something almost farcical about the scene as the smelly old man scuttled out of the grey ruins and dodged and staggered towards the steep shelf of rock, while stumbling, heavy-footed constables tried to apprehend him. The noise skittered across the moorland like a bird in flight, reaching up to the curtains of warm air, echoing under the rock, but it ended briefly when Shuffler gained a ledge under a long overhang and perched there like a great bald-headed vulture.

The policemen paused, breathlessly, Shuffler watched them through a drunken haze, and the silence of the moor mingled with the drifting whisper of life windborne from the dales.

'Don't be a fool, Shuffler, come on down and you won't get hurt.'

Imprecations and obscenities and a black greasy can followed; the police stormed the ledge with a frontal assault. A nose bled, two helmets were sent flying, men crashed down through the pliant whipping ribs of scrub below the ledge, and suddenly it was all over and Shuffler was a pathetic, smelly old man, whispering and whimpering on the hot moor while burly policemen swore and sweated and frogmarched him to the squad cars on the road, almost a mile away.

Once in the car sleep took him rapidly; on the drive back to Crow's headquarters he was heard to murmur several times in his beery doze, 'All coppers is bastards.'

He still stuck to the same creed when he was finally roused and sobered at the station. It took the best part of two hours to do it; the number of beer cans littering the ruin he had inhabited bore testimony to the splendour of the binge he had undertaken. Crow wondered where he had got the money from, but one of the cans thrown in a drunken rage at the constables produced eight pounds, so it was obvious that Shuffler had been saving for a beery day. Now he had had it he wanted only to sleep, but the bastard coppers were not prepared to allow him that luxury.

Crow questioned Shuffler at length. For almost an hour the old tramp refused even to speak to him, and Crow had to leave the interview room twice in order to get a breath of fresh air. Shuffler could not have bathed in a year. The thought finally gave Crow an idea and he threatened the tramp with just that – a bath. Shuffler immediately became much more cooperative, if still somewhat surly, and finally Crow obtained the information he desired.

It amounted to a confirmation of his suspicions.

'I seed him up on a hill one day and I was short of a bit of cash so I tapped him as I went by. He was sitting there just staring out over the country, and he seemed a reasonable gent and he gave me thirty pence. Then he got chattin', and he sort of asked me about the moor, and the lonely places and so on, and I tol' him about Lockyer's Tarn, how it was gloomy and sort of creepy and all that, and he started to laugh like he was pleased about something. Never saw him again.'

It was then that Crow took Shuffler down to see the corpse of Erich Schulman.

The water had bloated Schulman's features until he looked ten years older than he had been. The skin was grey and puckered, and on the slab the body looked obscene. Shuffler staggered as he saw Schulman and to Crow's surprise started to cry. He would not have thought the old tramp was capable of sentiment, but it was not until they got back to the room that he realized the tears had been occasioned not by sentiment but fear. In the face of the dead man on the slab Shuffler had seen his own face.

It loosened his tongue, nevertheless. He was suddenly old and vulnerable and pathetically eager to please. He gave Crow rambling details of the conversation with Schulman, and he told Crow how in June Charles Rutland had come scrambling up to his hut and waved money in his face.

'He said he wanted information. Asked me about a foreign chap who'd spoken to me on the hill, asked what he'd wanted. I didn't tell him at first but he waved a fiver in my face and in the end I told him. I told him I'd mentioned Lockyer's Tarn to the foreign chap – that man down there on the slab – and he seemed excited and pleased. And when he shoved some money in my hand I told him the rest, how a couple of nights later I'd been on the moor and I'd seen lights at the Tarn, car lights, but when I went down to the tarn in the dawn there was no car there. And no tracks runnin' away, either. Aw, I know I didn't tell you before, but I didn't know that foreign chap was in the tarn, did I? And that Rutland feller, he gave me money. And coppers–'

'Is bastards,' Crow said. 'And you don't tell them anything unless you have to.'

When Shuffler left the station his head was bent and his shoulders dejected. He seemed to be crying again.

The next twenty-four hours were spent in consultation with Wilson, going over ground familiar to both men, checking facts and details, building up a dossier on Conrad Gunther, marshalling facts into logical patterns, preparing a case against the German businessman that would look watertight if brought to court.

Crow still felt somewhat uneasy about some aspects of the case and pressed Wilson to make further contact with Interpol in the hope that more definite evidence of a link between Gunther and Grunfeld could be brought to light. In particular he wanted to check what Rutland had described as 'photo and signature correspondence'. But once again they drew a blank. The answer from Interpol was that no signature remained on record, and there was no extant photograph of Grunfeld that could in any way prove useful.

Crow found it puzzling. He made several calls to Scotland Yard, but once again there seemed to be a remarkable paucity of information on Grunfeld – while Conrad Gunther, in spite of being a public figure, seemed to have courted little publicity.

Crow was determined, nevertheless, to press ahead.

He appreciated there were dangers in making an approach to Conrad Gunther, especially at this particular point of time when the man was in England for business reasons, but Crow had never been a man to back away from a problem.

Shuffle at it sideways, he thought with a

wry grin, but back away, never. He wanted answers.

Next day, in London, he got them.

2

Commander Bill Gray waved a confident hand as Crow came into his room at Scotland Yard, and grinned. He was a handsome, burly man of forty with thick curly brown hair untouched by the frost of age. He was endowed with a nervous energy that found expression in his hands and eyes; neither were ever still. He was a controlled person, nevertheless, and Crow knew that there were occasions when his considerable reserves of tact and diplomacy were called upon to good effect in dealing with the expectations of the office and the workload of his men. Crow respected him as a professional, and as a man – even liked him to a certain degree – but he was not Crow's kind of man. There was always a hint of reserve in Crow's attitude towards Bill Gray, an unwillingness to go all the way to meet him. It was something Crow was not entirely able to explain even to himself: perhaps it was a simple enough matter, however. Possibly it was just that Crow didn't trust Gray. Crow had a job to do and did it. He saw things clearly.

Commander Bill Gray didn't – or to be fair, *couldn't*. There had been one occasion, in the Marlin case, when Gray had wanted Crow to pull out, hold back on certain enquiries he had wanted to make. Crow had never forgotten it, and never forgiven Gray. He smiled carefully now as Gray boomed out a welcome.

'Come in, John, come in and sit down.'

He jerked his head towards the window. 'Damn English weather. Heat, then a cold wind like this one. Makes me shiver. It would have made you shiver if you'd been up on the Yorkshire moors today, wouldn't it?'

'Yes, sir, it would.'

Gray sat down. The shortness and coolness of Crow's reply seemed to have passed unnoticed. He jerked a pipe out of his jacket pocket, lit it and sat puffing it for a moment. His eyes were lidded heavily, and Crow could make nothing out of his tone of voice when Gray said, 'I hear you found another body up there.'

'That's right. A man called Erich Schulman. He'd been shot, left in the back of the car, which was then pushed into the tarn from the top of a crag and he's been...'

'Decaying.' Gray said precisely, and clamped his teeth on his pipe in a vicious grin. 'You've been carrying out various checks with Interpol and the Yard.'

'That's right.'

'Like to tell me about it?'

Crow hesitated. Gray was staring at him now, but his eyes were expressionless.

'Not particularly. There are still loose ends. I don't see much point–'

'I do. I like to be kept in the picture.'

Crow's tone was as firm and controlled as Commander Gray's. 'I'm a member of the Murder Squad. I'm in charge of the investigation into Rutland's murder. This second killing had obvious links with Rutland. I'm reluctant to talk it over with you at this stage until–'

'I wish you would, John. I wish you'd tell me *all* about it, and what leads you have.'

Anger moved in John Crow's chest. He fought it because he knew what anger could do to him. There were few occasions when he permitted himself the luxury of emotion and they were normally private occasions: when emotions, particularly the violence of anger, intruded upon his professional life, he felt helpless, vulnerable, for it could affect his efficiency and his professionalism.

He could not afford anger when he was doing a job. He clenched his bony fists and sat more upright in his chair.

'All right. I'll tell you what I have – and I hope you'll then extend me the courtesy of explaining why you want to know. From the investigations I've carried out so far with Detective-Inspector Wilson and the local police, I've come to certain conclusions.'

Gray smiled, but it was a professional smile that held little meaning; it was meant to mollify, but the iron hand would still be within the glove. 'You're making this sound very official, John.'

'I think it's safer that way,' Crow said stiffly. 'We discovered that Charles Rutland was murdered, the weapon used, a poker. He died about three in the morning. It looks as though he was expecting company; he was attacked by a man called Orchard, who left the door open. The killer then came in through the open door and finished the job. I believe the man who killed Rutland did so because Rutland was blackmailing him ... or his employer.'

He paused. Something flickered in Gray's eyes, but he said nothing. After a moment, Crow continued. 'Further investigations disclosed that Rutland had met a foreigner –

Erich Schulman – a few weeks earlier. Schulman was murdered. Rutland went looking for the body, found its location, then he too was murdered. Our deduction from these events is that the same man killed both Schulman and Rutland – because both men were involved in the same action.'

'And what was that action?' Gray asked softly.

'They intended blackmailing a German businessman called Conrad Gunther.'

Gray grimaced suddenly, and put down his pipe. It lay on the table before him and he stared at it, watching the smoke wreathe upwards. His handsome face was marked with doubt and indecision. He sighed.

'I think you're barking up the wrong tree, John.' Crow was silent and Gray shuffled uneasily in his seat. He looked up and candour shone from his eyes, as insincere as a Judas kiss.

'I would advise no further investigations along these lines. You'd be wasting your time.'

'The facts we have–'

'Facts are like statistics, John, you know that. They can be made to prove anything you've a mind to, if you use them right. All I'm saying is, look elsewhere.'

'Not at Gunther?'

The words were a naked challenge and Gray knew it. He pondered over their directness and force, the aggression with which Crow had almost spat them out, and he was worried, but he stuck to his point.

'Listen to me, John. There are occasions ... a jack in the field, he sees things, picks up information, makes deductions which look *right*, but he suffers from one infirmity – involvement. He's there, he wants a villain, he *uses* facts at his disposal to finger that villain, but in so doing he loses something. Objectivity. We all know cases where there are so many facts we can't see wood for trees. There are other cases where everything points to one man – but it could be that objectivity would point elsewhere. Now me, I sit here in a chair in London and I watch you fellows digging around and I can see you're doing a damn good job but I'm not *involved* like you are. And I retain my objectivity. On this case...'

'No.' Crow's voice was harsh, and he was aware that his cheeks would be white now, making him look more than ever like a death's head. 'This has nothing to do with objectivity.'

Gray licked his lips. 'All right, I'll meet you part of the way on that. The fact is, I *know* you're wrong, because facts have come to me–'

'*What facts?*'

The room was silent. The colour began to retreat from Gray's face; he didn't like Crow's tone and his own temper was rising. 'I don't intend disclosing them to you, even if I were at liberty to do so. I'm simply advising you that nothing will be gained by pressing issues on Conrad Gunther. The information I have–'

'Information, hell!' Crow sneered. His anger was getting the better of him and he was unable to hold back the words. 'It's not information you're talking about, it's pressure, political pressure! Gunther is over here on business and he's talking to the Government, so some damn' Minister has got wind of the fact I want to talk to Gunther, and he and some damn' civil servant and you too, for all I know, have got the shakes in case I upset some political applecart! You don't even know what I've got on Gunther, but you want to discount it right from the start. This is a *murder* investigation, damn it, and you're not going to tell me to pull back. You can try, but you'll have to give me the push to make me do it.'

'I'm strong enough to give you the push,

John,' Gray said coldly. 'Don't overplay your hand.'

'Is there another man on the Murder Squad you could then manipulate? I doubt it. Whoever you used, in the end he'd come up with the same leads, the same questions. And he'd want to question Conrad Gunther!'

Bill Gray frowned. He began to drum his fingers on the desk. He seemed about to say something, then thought better of it. He picked up his pipe again, but did not smoke it; he stared at it as though he had never seen it before.

'So you won't take advice?'

Crow's silence convinced him. He glared at Crow, pressed a button on his desk and leaned back in his chair. 'All right, John,' he said, 'if that's the way you feel, you'd better tell me what you've got on Conrad Gunther.'

A door whispered open behind Crow's back. He did not turn to look at the person who entered, expecting him to come forward. He waited, looked at Gray, but Gray made no sign. Crow turned his head, looked back to the newcomer and saw him taking a chair at the back of the room. He intended sitting behind Crow.

He was no more than thirty years of age,

tall and slim. His fair hair was cut short. He had a narrow face with high cheekbones and his eyes were pale blue, intense in their colour and nervous energy. They were cold eyes and they regarded Crow dispassionately and without interest. Yet the man had come into the room at Gray's pressing of the button, and he had obviously entered to listen to what Crow had to say.

Crow glared at Gray, waited for him to effect an introduction. Gray showed no intention of doing so. 'Well?' he said.

Crow struggled with the anger that surged inside him. For a moment he thought of refusing to speak in front of the stranger, and then he swore to himself: if this is the way Gray wanted to play it, if he wanted to ignore this man in the room, Crow could go along with that.

'I'll be brief,' Crow said coldly. 'Charles Rutland worked for the scandal magazine, *Scathe*. He heard that Conrad Gunther was shortly coming to England to conduct certain talks at a fairly high level, and in order to get some background material on him, and possibly produce an embarrassing story – as you know, that's how *Scathe* works – he went to Germany.'

There was a slight shuffling movement

behind Crow: he paused, then ignored it.

'I think it's likely the original story to be used concerned Gunther's activities in Rhodesia. Certainly, this is what Earl Robson told me – Rutland was to investigate allegations that Gunther had carried on trade and negotiations with the Rhodesian Government while sanctions were still imposed by Britain and other countries. He would have exposed this in *Scathe;* it would have been an important story, in view of the circumstance of Gunther's arrival to talk here at Ministerial level.'

'There's no substance in this story, of course,' Gray commented smoothly.

'I have no interest in it,' Crow replied. 'Indeed, Rutland himself lost interest pretty soon after arriving in West Berlin, I imagine. Because he came across a bigger story. And because of that, he died.'

Gray's glance flickered past Crow to the man in the corner of the room; it was the first acknowledgment he had made of his existence.

'All right,' he said softly. 'Just what was the story that Rutland picked up?'

'I don't know all the details, but the basic fact is quite simple. The man we know as Conrad Gunther was not christened with that name. My guess is that Rutland was told the real Conrad Gunther died in North Africa during Rommel's campaign. His identity and papers were taken by another man, a Nazi, who used them to escape the Allies' net and make his way to South America, along the route so many Nazis used after 1944.'

'This sounds pretty far-fetched to me–'

'There's enough evidence to support the story,' Crow said quietly. He had regained control now and could speak almost dispassionately. 'The man who is now masquerading as Conrad Gunther is a Nazi war criminal called Grunfeld, Wilhelm Grunfeld. He has been sentenced to death *in absentia* by a French court. This is what Charles Rutland learned. This is why Charles Rutland died. Grunfeld, Gunther, call him what you will – he couldn't afford to let the truth emerge.'

A chair scraped behind Crow, and a moment later the man with the Slavic features came forward, placed his chair beside Gray's desk and sat down, facing Crow. He placed one elbow on the desk, looking at Gray, and then turned to observe Crow. His expression was friendly. 'I'm sure we can talk about this, iron out any misconceptions that have arisen.'

Crow ignored him and directed his question to Bill Gray. 'Who the hell is this?'

Gray made no reply. The fair-haired man at his side smiled coldly.

'My name is Dance.'

3

He took a pack of Turkish cigarettes from his pocket, offered them around, and, when both Gray and Crow refused, he lit one for himself, smoked it briefly, then regarded its glowing end in a somewhat theatrical manner.

'I wonder whether you'd be prepared to tell me on what grounds you make these ... ah ... suppositions, Inspector Crow?'

'I wonder on what grounds you think you have a right to ask me?'

Gray shuffled in his chair; this was going to be one of those occasions when his diplomacy and tact were to be called upon.

'I think Mr Dance had better be kept in the picture, John.'

'Why?'

Dance was smiling again, but it found no reflection in his eyes.

'Let's say I have an interest – a *professional* interest in Conrad Gunther.'

Crow hesitated, caught Gray's glance and read the plea in it, and shrugged. 'They are more than mere suppositions. Rutland kept notes in a pocket-book expenses for his trips, and so on. Amongst those notes were various queries concerning Gunther.'

'What sort of queries?'

'They concerned his adopted son, his date of birth, his appearance, his signature–'

'Did you carry out a check on these?' Dance interrupted swiftly.

'Yes. The results were largely negative – even Interpol couldn't help us.' Dance settled back in his chair with an expression that could be described only as satisfied. To prick his bubble Crow added, 'But we have enough on the first two queries to convince me Rutland was on to a real story.'

'Yes, but fact or fiction?'

'There's only one way of finding out,' Crow said.

Dance carefully flicked ash into the tray on the desk, and hesitated, choosing his words. 'I take it you want to interview Conrad Gunther, present him with these ... ah ... suppositions, and ask him questions about Rutland?'

'Yes.'

'He'll be able to tell you nothing.'

'Are you his keeper?'

Dance flickered an angry glance at Crow, but covered it almost immediately. He brought back the friendly smile. 'Something like that. Let me put it like this–' He waved a hand towards the silent Bill Gray. 'Let *us* put it like this. In our considered judgment there is nothing to be gained by your interviewing Conrad Gunther. What you have said ... well, I doubt if it's true, but in any case I assure you he has no knowledge of this man Rutland.'

'And I can't take that assurance. I need to find out for myself. I mean to see Gunther and ask him.'

Dance cocked his head to one side and looked almost apologetically towards Gray. He shrugged his shoulders as Gray leaned forward, placing broad hands palm down on the desk in front of him.

'It's not on, John,' he said. His voice was harsh and deliberate. 'You'll just have to take our word for it. Gunther can't help you. That's that. There'll be no interview.'

Crow's own tone was deceptively mild. 'You're wrong. I mean to see Gunther. It is essential to my investigation. You tried this on me once before, Commander, and on that occasion I did as I was told. Then, it was pressure from friends in high-up places.

I did it once, I won't do it again, even if politics and Ministers are concerned. I've got a job to do and I'll damned well do it even if toes do get trodden on. You try to stop me and I'll go upstairs–'

'They'll support me, John,' Gray warned.

Dance stubbed out his cigarette, half smoked. 'Gentlemen, gentlemen, let's not get excited over this. There's no reason why we should involve other people. It may be Inspector Crow isn't fully apprised of the background. You're probably not aware that Gunther is an important businessman who will be talking at the highest level concerning our machine-tools industry–'

'Mr Dance,' Crow said quietly, 'I know all that. And you won't scare me off as you did Earl Robson.'

It was a shot in the dark but it struck home; Dance blinked, then stared hard at Crow, considering. 'You're a very determined man, Inspector.'

'Determined, and *right*.'

Dance's gaze became tangled with thought; it was as though he were no longer seeing Crow but had turned his eyes inward, to seek out something within himself. He remained silent for almost a minute and Gray made no attempt to speak. Crow felt the pressure of that silence as though it were directed upon him, and yet Dance seemed almost to have forgotten there was anyone in the room with him. At last he stirred, however, glanced briefly at Gray and pursed his lips.

'I think you should leave us, Commander.'

Gray showed his surprise in his face; the surprise turned to resentment but his training bottled it up, held it back from expression. He nodded stiffly, rose, and left the room. Crow felt suddenly smaller than he had ever felt in his life: he had underestimated this man Dance. He had power; he was no mere civil servant. The realization did nothing to affect Crow's resolve, nevertheless.

'Let's just *assume* there's something in what you say,' Dance began quietly. 'About Gunther and Grunfeld being the same man, I mean. I could still assure you there's no connection with Rutland–'

'And I'd still ignore that assurance.'

Dance nodded, as though he had expected the remark. 'Blackmail, you intimated. What if I could show you such blackmail could never work?'

'How?'

Dance hesitated, thought for a moment and then reached a decision. 'I'm speaking hypothetically, of course. But let me take the case of a Nazi in Germany, trying to escape at the end of the war. A man like Grunfeld; a Gestapo man with knowledge of espionage and intelligence networks. I knew one such man – his story, that is. Do you know what happened? He was arrested, by the Americans, in Berlin, late in 1944.'

His fingers began to drum lightly on the table. 'It's true that there was a demand for the execution of this man – he was a criminal all right, but the Americans saw further than the immediate present. For this Nazi was a man of certain quality; he possessed a number of ... virtues, or what count for such in a Cold War. The Americans decided to make use of him, in the same way they made use of German scientists. They *recruited* him.'

Crow opened his mouth to speak, but thought better of it. Dance looked distinctly uneasy, but he continued speaking. 'This man began to work for the CIA; he handed over to them a great deal of information and agreed to act further in the intelligence network set up by the Americans. Let me say, he was well paid: he was not committed to Nazi ideology. His ideology was self-centred.' Dance stopped his finger drumming as though he had suddenly become aware of it. '*So* he worked for the CIA and Bonn Intelligence under an assumed name. He handed over to the CIA the names of prominent Frenchmen who had collaborated with the Gestapo during the Occupation. But a French court tried him *in absentia* and sentenced him to death: this proved somewhat embarrassing for the CIA so they gave him a forged passport, Red Cross documents, and money to get out of Germany. He used the international charitable Red Cross organization in Rome to get out of Europe, and then followed Eichmann's route to South America. But it didn't end there, Inspector.' Dance looked directly at Crow. His eyes were alive, glinting, but cold. 'This man built up a business for himself and married well, but he was always *active*, do you understand? He was still working for the CIA and Bonn. When he went to South Africa it was ostensibly to set up a business there: in fact, he founded a spy network to channel information back to Europe. Similarly, his Rhodesian unit was a cover for espionage again: and Britain had cause to be grateful for the work he did there. And if he *were* to visit England it would be to discuss with the Government matters other than mere business. You must remember, Inspector, a man such as I speak of is an *agent* first, a businessman second.' Dance leaned back in his chair and folded his arms. He remained silent for a moment as though waiting for Crow to appreciate the true import of his words. Then he said, 'A man like that is particularly susceptible, however, susceptible to rumour, and to having his cover blown. Rumour can be outfaced – the Rhodesians, for instance, suspected, might even have *known* he was acting as an agent in their country, but there was nothing they could do about it openly. But to have his identity questioned, to have it made public that he was once a Nazi, a war criminal,' Dance paused, and eyed Crow carefully. 'There are some who would say that such a man would have expiated his old sins by his actions since, in support of our Western democratic institutions.'

Crow smiled thinly. 'If you're asking me whether I subscribe to such a view you're wasting your time. It would be a complete irrelevancy. I'm investigating a murder – my personal feelings as to whether or not Grunfeld ... all right, your hypothetical Nazi if you so wish ... has expiated his sins are beside the point. They in no way influence me. I have a

209

job to do.'

'But I've explained–'

'No,' Crow interrupted. 'You've not explained. You said Gunther can't be involved, you assure me he isn't, and you suggested that blackmailing Gunther would never work. But you haven't explained why.'

Dance shook his head in a sudden exasperation and beat his left hand lightly against the table. 'Do you really want me to spell it out in words of one syllable ? All right, damn it, we're talking about Gunther. Can't you appreciate how *important* he is? He is the centre of an American and German-based intelligence network, and we wouldn't let a miserable piece of scum like Rutland put him on the spot – we wouldn't let Rutland get near to him.'

'But Rutland did,' Crow argued, 'and suborned one of Gunther's people as well. I believe that was when Gunther ordered–'

'But why should he make such an order?' Dance was losing his temper; in his view he had been behaving reasonably and sensibly, but Crow's refusal to see sense was annoying him considerably. He was not used to such behaviour. 'Can't you understand? Gunther wouldn't order this man Schulman to be killed; he wouldn't order Rutland to be murdered. *He wouldn't have to.'*

The words were out and his face became a mask immediately he realized just what they meant. He glared at Crow, but his eyes were cold in a dead face. His lips were tight, set thinly in a vicious line. Crow leaned forward and suddenly their roles were reversed. Dance had felt all along that he had the whip hand, but now their respective situations had changed. Crow almost felt a purr begin in his chest.

'Wouldn't have to?' he said. 'Does that mean what I suspect it does?'

Dance was silent.

'I've been assuming,' Crow continued, 'that Gunther got scared by Rutland and Schulman and so got rid of them both. I assumed he had the power and the money to hire a killer to do it for him. But you say...'

Dance's face moved, twitched, a sign of nervous anger in his cheek. But he still said nothing.

'Are you telling me that if Gunther had been bothered by Rutland,' Crow said, 'he would have told you, or one of your people? And the eradication of Rutland and Schulman would have been *your* job?'

Dance licked dry lips. His voice seemed slightly hoarse.

211

'I did not say—'

'Would it come under the head of political assassination?' Crow asked quietly. 'Wilhelm Grunfeld's cover must not be blown, so your department will ensure it is not. Earl Robson you scared off, but Rutland and Schulman—'

'No.' Dance stirred, put his hands on his knees, leaning forward as though about to spring. 'I knew nothing – the department was aware of nothing until Rutland died and your investigations started. No order to kill … no…' He seemed to be at a loss to choose the right phrase. 'I repeat,' he said at last, 'we were not involved until *after* Rutland's murder.'

'Then who did kill Rutland?' Crow asked deliberately. 'And who put Schulman in Lockyer's Tarn? You say Gunther could not have been involved, but if he is Wilhelm Grunfeld, let us think back to his background. It's one of violence and death. Are you sure, can you be *certain* that when Schulman left Germany and Rutland made his first demands, Conrad Gunther, or Wilhelm Grunfeld, would not have acted on his own behalf? You know *Gunther*, Mr Dance – but do you know *Grunfeld*?'

Dance was very still. He sat as though

carved from stone and his face was grey. No expression touched his features and he seemed to be looking through Crow, not seeing him, looking for a man from the past, a character he could not know, buried as it was in the dust of thirty years. But as the thought came to Crow, Dance shook himself, and the vagueness of his gaze was replaced with a cold wariness.

'You're causing me trouble,' he said.

'I don't give a damn,' Crow said pleasantly.

Dance nodded as though he knew it and pressed the button on Bill Gray's desk. A moment later the door opened and Commander Gray entered, rather surly, but diplomatic enough not to allow it to surface too clearly. Dance stood up, crisp, businesslike, losing no face by the firmness of his tone.

'I shall make arrangements for Inspector Crow to see Conrad Gunther,' he said. 'Today.'

Chapter 10

1

Dance was as good as his word.

Crow was impressed by the efficiency the man displayed. He was still not clear as to who Dance was, what his official position might be, and neither Dance nor Gray seemed prepared to tell him. But it was quite obvious that Dance possessed power, of a kind strong enough to silence Robson firmly and positively so that the Gunther story would never appear in *Scathe,* and of a kind sufficient to make speedy arrangements for an interview with Conrad Gunther.

Nor was Crow sufficiently immodest to allow himself the luxury of supposing that he had successfully held out against Dance, and bested him in an argument. Dance's job had been to head Crow off, prevent him from asking embarrassing questions of Gunther that the German might see as politically motivated, with a reason behind them – the wrecking of business negotiations or a

British Security operation against him and the CIA. Dance had undertaken that task and tried to head Crow away from Gunther, but during the conversation Dance had been forced to come face to face with his own doubts. There was just the possibility that Gunther would not have enlisted the support of Dance's Department or the CIA in eliminating the threat posed by Charles Rutland. There was the possibility that Gunther had reverted to his position of thirty years ago and used violence to achieve an objective. Certainly Dance knew Conrad Gunther, but he had never known Wilhelm Grunfeld – and he had no way of knowing which character had surfaced when Rutland had started asking for money.

So he had decided to settle it in his own mind. His car came to Scotland Yard and whisked him and Crow to the Hilton where Gunther was staying. At three in the afternoon John Crow met Conrad Gunther.

Crow was not sure what he had expected, but he saw a heavy man in an expensive, well-cut suit. It was early, but Gunther had a large whisky in his hand, and it was soon obvious that he enjoyed the good things in life that went with his status – food, drink, his hotel suite. He was almost six feet in height and upright of bearing. His body was thickening now, but he would have been a handsome, striking figure in his youth.

He had lost little of his vitality. His hand-clasp was sure and firm, almost competitive in its strength. He had bright blue eyes that would burn with intensity when he faced an intractable problem. His hair was sandy, cut short, thinning at the crown, his features were clean-cut, though jowls now gathered to detract from the line of his jaw. His chin seemed a little lop-sided as he smiled on being introduced to Crow, and Crow remembered what Wilson had told him about the facial characteristics of the Nazi, Wilhelm Grunfeld.

He was not fooled by the easy charming manner that Gunther displayed – the man would have qualities that could turn it into a cold hostility. But there were tired lines around his eyes, as though life was finally catching up with him, and the sag to his mouth when he wasn't thinking about his external appearance, the picture he pre-sented to the world, suggested that Conrad Gunther felt the strain of living as much as any man, if not more.

Crow saw it emerge during the course of their talk, but his first impression was one of strength.

'A drink?' Gunther said, smiling. 'No? The old police argument, never when working. You think I would thus corrupt you, hey?'

His English was smooth, correct, with only the slightest trace of an American accent, overlaid with German syllables. He would have worked at it, over the years.

He turned, took a seat on the long settee under the window, and smiled again at Crow, exuding confidence and approachability, benign, bestowing favours.

'Now then, Mr Dance tells me you would like to speak to me about some investigation that you are conducting. I am not at all clear how I can assist you, but be assured–'

'I am investigating the murder of Charles Rutland,' Crow said coldly.

Gunther scratched at his eyebrow; the smile did not leave his face.

'As I say, I do not see how I can help you.'

'You've never heard of Rutland? He worked for *Scathe* magazine.'

The blue eyes became thoughtful, and a little frown appeared on Gunther's face as his smile faded.

'That rag... As I recall, it must be three months or more since my office received a request from *Scathe* for an interview. It was while I was in West Berlin.'

'Did you grant Rutland an interview?'

The smile came back fleetingly, as though accepting the quickness of the question and the trap it held.

'I did not say *Rutland* asked for an interview. I said *Scathe* magazine made the request. To be quite honest with you, Inspector, it may well have been Rutland who made the request, I do not know. The fact is I do not handle such minor matters – one of my secretaries would have dealt with it. The matter came to my attention only as a matter of routine: the request was passed through to me with advice from my secretary that an interview would not be wise, and I accepted that advice.'

'Why was it thought not wise?'

'My dear Inspector,' Gunther said with a sigh, 'I receive many such requests. If I were to accept them all... As it is, I accept only those which are serious, are likely to be of benefit to my interests, or which are helpful to my image. Is that so wrong?'

Crow shook his head.

'You run your own life and business. But you say one of your secretaries handled the matter. Would that secretary be named Schulman?'

The frown was deeper now and more pronounced. It carved a deep line between his eyes, drew his brows together as Gunther hid his thoughts and kept his counsel for a moment.

'I can't answer that immediately,' he said at last.

'Can you find out?'

'My private secretary, Steiner, can probably check it.'

'I'd be grateful if he would.'

Steiner was South African by birth and he had retained his guttural accent. He was swift and efficient in his administration. Within a matter of minutes he came into the room with a file which he placed before Conrad Gunther. Gunther read it carefully then looked up.

'Your sources of information are to be respected, Inspector. Erich Schulman ... one of the assistant secretaries in my entourage, he was the man who passed on the request and who had the task of explaining to *Scathe* that I was not available. You know this? Or was it merely an inspired guess?'

His eyes were suddenly harder as they stared at Crow, blue water turning to ice.

'Let's say it was a guess inspired by certain facts in my possession.'

'Concerning Erich Schulman?' Crow nodded.

'He's dead.'

'I'm sorry to hear that.' The indifference in Gunther's tone belied his words. 'But if this man Rutland saw only one of my minor officials, I suppose there's little point in prolonging this interview, is there?'

He placed his hands flat on the settee as though about to rise, and glanced at Dance. The man made no move from his seat but said, 'I think Chief Inspector Crow will argue otherwise, Herr Gunther.'

Gunther looked at Crow again, with an arithmetical eye, summing him up. He was suddenly more wary, more aware.

'This does not finish the interview?' he said softly.

Crow's reply was harshly phrased.

'I'm afraid not. I should have said, a moment ago, guesswork based upon facts in my possession, concerning Erich Schulman ... and Wilhelm Grunfeld.'

The room remained silent for almost a minute. Gunther sat staring at Crow and his face was completely impassive save for a muscle in his cheek that jerked spasmodically, twice. But there was something else about his face, something almost indefinable: it was as though carved in stone it had weathered years of attack, but suddenly, at last, the first signs of erosion were appearing, a crumbling, a crack in the stone. Gunther's features did not change, Crow could have sworn to that, yet something happened to them. When he spoke at last, the word came out as though fogged with sleep.

'Dance?'

The security agent stirred in his chair and said impassively, 'I tried to explain. He insisted. Eventually, I decided you'd better see him, listen to his questions.'

A cynical smile twitched at Gunther's mouth.

'And answer them?'

Dance made no reply but sat very still. Gunther's eyes cleared, indecision vanished, and he leaned back, folded his arms and said, 'All right, Inspector, I don't know what you want but I'll listen, at least.'

Crow hesitated, suddenly uncertain of his ground.

Gunther had been disturbed by Grunfeld's name, but was now in control and at ease. Crow decided to face the citadel with a frontal attack.

'There are certain similarities between you and a Gestapo officer called Wilhelm Grunfeld who was sentenced to death in 1951 and has never been located.'

'My name is Conrad Gunther,' the businessman said softly.

'You adopted the son of Wilhelm Grunfeld.'

'There was nothing illegal in that.'

'There are other coincidences–'

'As you say. Coincidences.'

Crow glared at Gunther. He was getting nowhere. He decided to start again.

'Did you ever meet Rutland?'

'No.'

'What was your reaction when he tried to blackmail you?'

Gunther laughed; it contained a note of genuine amusement that Crow did not like.

'Blackmail? Me? I have received no threats from this man Rutland. I had no knowledge of his existence until you came to speak to me here today. *Scathe* magazine wanted to interview me, yes; Rutland worked for them, you tell me. But blackmail – really, Inspector!'

The contempt in his voice goaded Crow, and on the verge of losing his temper he said, 'So you deny any complicity in the deaths of Charles Rutland and Erich Schulman, as your friend Dance has denied complicity?'

Gunther glanced swiftly at Dance and something seemed to pass between them. It could have been a question, but the answer from Dance was certainly a negative, and when Gunther turned back to Crow his confidence remained.

'I deny it completely, Inspector – indeed, I'm not even sure I know what you're talking about. Er ... *do* you?'

Crow caught himself, he recognized the deliberation behind the remark and knew that Gunther wanted him to lose his temper. The realization made him hold back, turned his anger to icy determination. He suddenly wanted Gunther, and intended getting him.

'Perhaps it would help you realize my position, Herr Gunther ... or whatever your true name is, if I told you what I do know.'

Gunther appreciated the mildness of Crow's tone; Crow felt he almost experienced a certain pleasure. Perhaps Gunther liked an adversary; he had met enough in his lifetime to want to sharpen himself on another.

'I think that would be as well, Inspector. Then I shall be able to point to the errors in your ... deductions.'

'Then I will start with Charles Rutland's visit to West Berlin,' Crow said smoothly. 'He wanted an article on you for *Scathe;* it would have been muck-raking, of course, for that was *Scathe's* way, but while researching into your background, Rutland unearthed certain interesting coincidences concerning you and Wilhelm Grunfeld. He failed to obtain his interview, but in the course of his attempts he made the acquaintance of Erich Schulman, one of your secretaries.'

'I agree with this, I have said so,' Gunther said brusquely, nodding.

'Disappointed though he may have been, Rutland discovered Schulman could be useful. As one of your secretaries he knew your organization and was able to help fill in some background material on you. He convinced Schulman there was money to be made in blackmailing you, so Schulman left your employ and came to England–'

'He gave no notice,' Gunther said sharply, staring at the file, 'but took leave, from which he did not return. According to this he is missing–'

'He's been lying at the bottom of Lockyer's Tarn,' Crow said.

Gunther looked again at Dance, frowned, and turned back to Crow.

'How did this happen?'

Crow smiled grimly.

'I can provide some guesswork to go with a number of facts. Rutland discovered you were really Grunfeld and decided to blackmail you. He enlisted Schulman–'

'Schulman was a minor cog and could know nothing damaging to me,' Gunther said, shaking his head. He raised no argument about his connection with the name Grunfeld, however, and Crow realized he felt safe in Dance's presence, even to make such semi-admissions. Dance would never allow Crow to speak of them outside this room.

'He intended blackmailing you with Schulman's help,' Crow repeated doggedly. 'They decided it was necessary to get Schulman to a safe place: Yorkshire was thought suitable. Schulman went there, stayed at a pub called the Three Bells under an assumed name and was contacted there by Rutland.'

'If he used an assumed name–'

'He registered under the name of Romanoff, but we know Romanoff and Schulman are one. The corpse has been identified.'

Gunther seemed about to speak, then thought better of it. He glanced swiftly at the file, frowned and then grimaced.

'Please go on, Inspector,' he said courteously.

'Once contacted, Schulman moved into a

bungalow Rutland had rented for the purpose. He lay low there while Rutland went back to Germany to finalize his blackmail plans – but things went wrong. You had reacted swiftly–'

'Reacted?'

'You sent a man to Yorkshire to deal with Schulman.'

Gunther was silent for a moment. Again he glanced at Dance and the security agent shook his head. Grimly, Gunther asked Crow to go on.

'Schulman was careless. He was contacted by your man and a meeting-place arranged. Schulman wanted somewhere open and quiet, and an old tramp suggested such a place when he asked him for a lonely spot. Schulman told Rutland, probably over the phone, that he had spoken to this tramp. It was the last time Rutland spoke to Schulman.'

'And what exactly happened?' Gunther asked in a quiet voice.

'Your man stole a car from Leeds, drove to meet Schulman, killed him, put him in the stolen car and pushed the car into Lockyer's Tarn.'

'Very dramatic.'

Crow ignored Gunther's ironic tone.

'Rutland came back, not knowing what had happened to Schulman and needing him to prove his story about you. There was only one lead he had – the tramp, who had casually mentioned a place to Schulman. There was some difficulty in tracing the tramp, but Rutland found him, learned about the tarn. And the blackmail was on again – for murder. And this time a *recent* murder, not one thirty years old.'

Gunther did not like the last remark. His eyes were ice-cold, his mouth a thin, angry line. Perhaps he believed the argument Dance had mentioned, that a man could live down his past. In Crow's book Wilhelm Grunfeld could never live down such a past, for he was still living it, under a different guise, for a different overlord. The motivations remained the same – self-interest.

'This story is preposterous.'

'No. Most of it can be proved. When you realized Rutland was going to continue with his threats, you agreed, probably through an intermediary, to meet him. Rutland was excited by the prospect: he saw himself in money. *Blood* money. He visited a woman that night – she testifies to his strange, excited mood. He left her, returned to the bungalow, waited for the messenger. But someone else got there first – the common-law husband of the woman Rutland had been sleeping with. This man beat Rutland badly, left him unconscious. It was easy for your man, Gunther, easy for him to step through the open doorway, pick up a poker and finish the job. And the threats were over – Schulman was dead, Rutland was dead, your secret was safe.'

'But it wasn't, was it?' Gunther said. An angry gleam lit his eyes and his mouth twisted viciously. 'How can you say it was safe when *you* are here now?'

'I–'

'Dance, you should be able to save me from fools such as this man!' Gunther said, ignoring Crow.

Dance stared at him, then lifted one shoulder.

'I had to be sure. And you have made no answer to the charges Chief Inspector Crow makes.'

Gunther stared at him in open disbelief. He snorted, almost laughed, but his anger was too strong to permit of amusement.

'You don't think he can *prove* my involvement? Damn him, he has a few facts, and a fertile imagination supplies the rest. You can't honestly believe I would ever place myself in the situation–'

'I have no doubt you will wish to deny–' Crow began.

Gunther turned on him swiftly, like a spitting cat.

'Deny what? This rubbish you raise? I need to deny nothing. The theory is full of holes. In the first place Erich Schulman was a minor employee of mine. No information could have come into his possession which this man Rutland could have used. He knew *nothing*. Secondly, if ever this situation had arisen I would not have acted – I would have asked *others* to intervene.'

Both Crow and Dance knew who he meant, and Dance stirred in his chair. It was the answer he had hoped to hear: Gunther, faced with the problem, would have relied on his department. He looked at Crow enquiringly. Crow was not convinced, Gunther had so much to lose, and yet logic suggested that Gunther would not have needed to act on his own.

'Schulman–'

'Schulman, Schulman,' Gunther snapped testily, 'who is this man Schulman? You are pathetic in your attempts, Inspector. You follow a series of *non sequiturs*. Rutland seeks an interview with me, Schulman meets him,

Schulman dies, Rutland dies, Schulman was employed by me ... so you think I killed them both? Why? *I tell* you *they never approached* me with *threats*. And who were they? A minor journalist attached to a spiteful, muck-raking rag, and a petty clerk under the shadow of death – they were both better away from society. Neither deserved to live. Why bother yourself about them?'

It was an argument familiar to Crow; he had heard it during the Second World War. Gunther, for all his protests and recent activities, was still Wilhelm Grunfeld. Dance knew it too, but his face remained impassive at Gunther's outburst. Crow bit back a retort, nevertheless, for there was something else...

'You said Schulman was under the shadow of death?'

'An expression,' Gunther said disgustedly, waving a hand and standing up, the file tucked under his arm. 'But what did you mean by it?' Crow insisted. Gunther's eyes narrowed, and the hint of a smile, bitter and vicious, touched his lips. He took the file in his left hand, tapped it against his right.

'You mean you have not researched into Erich Schulman the way you have researched into Conrad Gunther?'

Crow remained silent and the smile on Gunther's face broadened, became even more unpleasant.

'You lack the thoroughness of my race, Inspector Crow. This name Schulman registered under in Yorkshire ... *Romanoff?* He, or perhaps Rutland, had a macabre sense of humour. The reason is here on my file. Is it not on yours?'

Contemptuously, he tossed the file towards John Crow.

'Did you not know Erich Schulman was a sick man?'

2

It took Crow almost two days to get clear of London. First of all he spent several hours with Dance and two civil servants who emphasized the necessity for all rumours and whispers about Gunther to be killed. Painstakingly they went over the names of all personnel at Leeds and York who had been connected with the investigation into Rutland's death and examined the extent to which they might have become apprised of the connection between Gunther and Grunfeld. There were at least six people, and telephone orders were given for them to be checked by Dance's department. Crow was given the distinct impression that his activities had seriously jeopardized proceedings of moment, and that a mere murder investigation should not have been allowed to interfere with business of the kind Gunther was indulging in.

Doggedly, Crow stuck to his guns. He received no reward for his persistence in the matter. Commander Gray reported, not without some satisfaction, that there was bound to be trouble about it, and thought that Gunther would probably call off the conference in London and return to Germany.

Crow's own investigations further held him in London. He used Scotland Yard to make enquiries into the details he found in Gunther's file on Erich Schulman, but in the end he discovered he was still lacking vital corroborative evidence.

Then he remembered the Chief Constable, and he returned to Yorkshire.

'I don't like it,' the Chief Constable grumbled. 'I don't see why it had to be here. I don't like getting involved on a personal basis – far better to get him down to the station, or see him at his home and question him there.'

'I don't want it so official,' Crow replied. 'Not until I'm sure. This way is better.'

'That may be so but this is my club and I don't like...' The Chief Constable's voice died away in a grumbling. Crow knew that one of the reasons he was upset was that he had not been told very much about why Crow wanted to meet Harry Field here at the club, or what lay behind the investigation. There would be time enough to tell him later, if Crow learned what he hoped to learn.

They sat in the lounge of the club, a short flight of stairs above the main entrance hall, and with a view of the magnificent marble staircase that the wool merchants of Bradford had built out of their nineteenth-century profits in an attempt to match the Victorian elegance of the London clubs they had seen during their business visits south. Crow thought they would have been better employed creating something for themselves rather than aping the faded idiom of a dead era, but this was obviously what they wanted.

'Here he is now,' the Chief Constable said, and heaved himself out of his chair with a grunt to extend a welcoming hand towards Harry Field. The man came up the steps into the lounge, smiling; he was tall, about fifty years old, with a shock of white hair, and grey eyes that seemed faded, looking out as they did from a face tanned with sun other than that enjoyed on the Yorkshire moors. His handgrip was firm, and though he blinked when he took in the details of Crow's appearance, he did not allow his glance to linger.

'Are you gentlemen drinking?'

'We waited for you,' the Chief Constable said, and Field raised a hand to the waiter standing near the door. He ordered three whiskies, settled back in his chair and smiled around.

'Not often I get the chance to meet two bigwigs from the police force. Mind, in the wool business we don't get much truck with the law – there's a bit of rustling on the moors but nothing serious. Nothing to involve Scotland Yard, anyway. You're investigating the Rutland murder, aren't you, Inspector? And I hear they dredged someone out of Lockyer's Tarn, too.'

'That's right.' Crow nodded, paused and said, 'At the moment we're trying to check out all the details ... you'll have heard, perhaps, that the body in the tarn was found in a car.'

Field pulled a face.

'So I heard. Aileen Selby's car too, by damn. Hell of a shock for her, I expect. Not the sort of thing you want to be involved in when you're making preparations for your daughter's wedding. She's out there in Crete now – did you tell her about the Volvo before she went?'

'Yes. She knows all about it.'

'Ah, well,' Field said cheerfully, 'I'm sure she won't allow it to interfere with her plans for Ingrid. Aileen Selby is a very able, very determined woman.'

'You know her quite well,' Crow said quietly.

Field looked at him, glanced towards the Chief Constable and then laughed outright.

'All right, you know about it, I expect. It wagged a few tongues at the time – Harry Field, crusty bachelor, prepared to forgo his trips to Austria and *après-ski* and all that sort of stuff, to take the marital vows – and at his age too. Yes, I know, it was the talk of the Exchange but I didn't give a damn. And I don't mind saying I'd marry her now – if she'd have me.' He broke off as the waiter approached and handed the drinks to the three men. When he had gone, Field grinned. 'But the thing is, she won't, will she?'

He did not seem disturbed by the fact of his rejection. Crow suspected that he might even have been a little relieved: prepared to marry Mrs Selby he might have been, but it may well have also raised doubts in his mind about the loss of his bachelorhood.

'You've known her a long time, haven't you?' Crow asked.

'Longer than I care to mention,' Field said, and sipped his whisky. 'I first met her when we were both little more than kids – she'd just moved to Sydney, I recall, and was living in the next block. Went to school with her – she was called Aileen Fellowes then. Scrawny kid, but she really blossomed later. But I left Sydney at the end of the war and came across here. Biggest surprise of my life when she turned up here in Bradford one day – a widow! And she'd been married to Selby and living nearby and I never knew! It's a small world, I said, and gave her a hug.'

He shook his head ruefully.

'And now her daughter's marrying Chris Santer. Time goes, don't it? Ingrid, she looks very much like her mother did, all those years ago. Makes you think…'

'How old were you when you left Australia?' Crow asked.

'Hell, young, young, early twenties–'

'And Aileen Selby?'

Field stared at Crow in surprise.

'Nineteen, I suppose.' He glanced at the Chief Constable. 'You didn't exactly tell me why you wanted a chat–'

'I'd be very grateful if you would offer your assistance,' Crow said firmly, 'and speak frankly. I have been making a number of enquiries and it may well be you can resolve some problems. I don't feel I can give you information, but if you could answer my questions, however inconsequential or personal they seem to be...'

Field frowned. He seemed uncertain, but then he shrugged and pulled a face.

'Fire away.'

'Do you remember the last time you saw Aileen Selby – or Aileen Fellowes – before you left Sydney?'

'Ahuh. Couple of weeks before I took the boat.'

'And did you hear anything about her after that time?'

Field frowned again, then glared thoughtfully at his glass.

'How do you mean?'

'You'd come to England. You had family

back in Sydney? Did they ever mention Aileen Fellowes to you in their letters?'

Field hesitated, and a certain reluctance crept into his voice.

'Well, yes, I suppose they did. I mean, I *had* just come to England and the family sort of kept me in touch for a few years – while it still seemed important to know about school friends and so on. After a while, of course, one changes...'

'Do you remember them saying anything specific about Aileen Fellowes?'

'It was a long time ago,' Field muttered.

'But was there anything?' Crow persisted. He had the impression Harry Field did recall something from that time, but was not keen to talk about it. 'I realize that it might be personal, but, believe me, I need to know.'

Field shook his head.

'I'm not sure ... it's all rather a long time ago and I'm not even certain whether I can remember it properly. A chap forgets ... and there's also the fact that it could only have been rumour at the time, and you know how rumour gets inflated...'

'But there was something about Aileen Fellowes.'

'I ... I suppose there was. Nothing much really. What it all boils down to is she wanted to get married.'

'And?'

'And her parents didn't approve. Her father, John Fellowes, was the manager of a small engineering company, and I suppose he had certain pretensions. He didn't approve of her choice and there was some trouble.'

'What sort of trouble?' Crow asked.

Field wrinkled his brow and concentrated.

'Well, as far as I remember, and it's only second-hand, mind, and there's no way I can check the accuracy of my memory now, but it seems to me I was told Aileen tried to force her parents' hands. She wanted to get married, they refused permission, so she tried to force them into agreeing.'

'How?'

Field scratched nervously at his hair.

'Now look, you've got to remember, I'm talking about *impressions* right now. Nothing specific was said by my family – they just hinted at a delicate subject and I just gained an ... impression. But it boils down to this. I think Aileen Fellowes ... slept with this chap she wanted to marry. Tried to shame her parents into agreement.'

'I see. And what happened then?'

'Far as I know, nothing. I'm not too clear about it but she didn't marry the guy, that's for sure, but whether it was because her old man still wouldn't wear it ... although now I think back I believe there was more to it than that. Something else occurred, Aileen went off the man or something... Anyway, I'm afraid that's all I can tell you. It's not much. And I don't know why you want to know. I mean, hell, it's a long time ago, and all it was, well, it was just a young girl's infatuation, wasn't it?'

'Maybe so.' Crow paused, considering, and eyed Harry Field. 'You said something else occurred. Did you gain any "impression" at the time as to what that might have been?'

Field's brow was clouded with doubt. Slowly he shook his head.

'I know there was some sort of blow-up, a scandal, maybe... Now wait a minute.' His eyes began to shine as memory bit, sharpened the edges of recall. 'A baby. That was it. My mother never exactly used that *word*, you understand, but that was it, Aileen slept with this guy and she had a kid. Sure, I remember now. Funny–' he frowned again, musing about the past – 'I met her up here, we talked over old times, I even got around to proposing and I had all but forgotten that. Not that it would've made a difference, you understand, but the things a guy forgets... But that was it. She had a kid. Didn't seem to make no difference, though – she didn't marry the father. When she did hitch up, it was to John Selby, some years later in England.'

'She didn't bring up the child?'

'Can't say. Don't know anything about the kid. I lost touch after that, I mean, my parents died, and I wasn't in direct contact anyway with other people back home. She certainly didn't mention the kid when I took her out here.'

'What sex was the child?'

'I tell you, I don't know.'

'Mr Field, I've carried out checks with the authorities in Australia, in Sydney, but this didn't come to light. It's why I came to you. It's as though the whole thing happened ... surreptitiously.'

Field shrugged, unable to help.

'What was the father's name?' Crow asked.

'I can't remember, not now, if I ever did know.'

'Why did Aileen's father disapprove of him ... I mean, what was there about the man?'

Field hesitated again.

'Well, it's a kind of a strange story, as I recall it. And you got to remember the

242

climate of the times. John Fellowes was of English stock and he was a pretty fierce patriot, you know. As far as I got it from my mother, what happened was this. In 1939 Sydney was one of the port of calls for a new idea – an international youth orchestra that was doing a sort of world tour. When the war broke out, the orchestra – it consisted of young lads and girls – was playing Sydney and it caused all sorts of problems because lots of these kids couldn't get home. So homes for most of them were found in town – they stayed, lots of them, grew up there, became Aussies. Others went home end of the war. But there was one group in the orchestra that caused trouble, problems, if you know what I mean. They were German.'

He frowned, glaring at Crow as though he were responsible for the attitudes he spoke of.

'It's rough, visiting the sins of the Nazis upon young kids but there you are. A lot of people who were prepared to take in young-sters balked at taking in Germans. And some of the kids were fourteen, fifteen, almost adults. Couldn't speak English, some of them. They had a kind of uneasy life, you can guess. Again, some of them settled, became Aussies. Others...'

243

'And Aileen Selby?' Crow asked softly.

'It seems she fell for one of these German lads and in 1945 she wanted to marry him. Her old man blew his top. I don't know whether it was just because the lad was a German, or whether the lad was a bit *too* German. Thing was, he clamped down, so it seems Aileen went with the boy, tried to force things. But, in the end, nothing came of it.'

'That's not strictly true,' Crow said. 'There was the baby, after all.'

Field shrugged.

'And you can't remember the name of the German boy?' Crow asked.

'No. I believe he didn't stay in Australia, I believe he went back to Germany end of the war, but ... well, if you were to suggest his name, there's no guarantee I'd recognize it, remember it from my mother's letters.'

'Let's try the name Schulman,' Crow said quietly.

Wilson left the forensic report with Crow and went to make the necessary flight bookings. Crow took the report with him when he went in to see the Chief Constable in his office. The Chief Constable waved him to a chair, put his fingertips together and scowled at Crow over them.

'Perhaps you'd now like to tell me what it's all about.'

'I haven't got the complete picture yet,' Crow said, 'but what I believe happened was that Aileen Fellowes had a child by a man called Schulman in Australia, and that Schulman named the boy Erich, and took him back to Germany. Erich Schulman grew up there and after his father died became an employee of Conrad Gunther. It was while working for Gunther that he met Charles Rutland. *Scathe* magazine wanted an expose on Gunther, but Rutland found a better, more *personal* story when he met an embittered and vicious Erich Schulman, a young man who wanted revenge. So Rutland saw the possibilities for blackmail, hatched the plot with Schulman, brought him to England–'

'Now wait a minute,' the Chief Constable said. 'What's this about blackmail? And revenge? You said Schulman was embittered–'

'Erich Schulman wanted revenge on his mother. He blamed her for his condition in life. I should have realized the truth sooner, I should have recognized the pointers. I'd been told that Rutland had a macabre sense of humour, but the use of the pseudonym

245

Romanoff when Schulman registered at the Three Bells apparently caused them both amusement, but it meant nothing to me – I wasn't *thinking*. Again, when Rutland was with Mrs Orchard he kept muttering and laughing over a phrase – *blood money*. I should have linked the two. I didn't. The fact was, Rutland wasn't using "blood money" as a term of art, in the conventional sense. He was putting his – and Schulman's – own personal meaning on it.'

He tapped the file on his knee.

'I now have Dr Frust's confirmation of information contained in Gunther's personal file on Erich Schulman. Schulman suffered from a particularly unpleasant blood disease – one which is suffered only by males, but *transmitted* by the females of the line.'

The Chief Constable was silent.

'Erich Schulman, like members of the Romanoff family,' Crow said heavily, 'was a haemophiliac.'

3

The water was a deep, painful blue, sharp as the colour of the sky, and the trim white sails of the yachts running out of the bay danced and fluttered like moths against a blue flame. On the slopes below her, bougainvillea flaunted its blooms, bright against the green of the hill, but closer to hand the crags and the rocks that crowned the ancient path glowered harsh and black in the afternoon sun.

Aileen Selby trained her field glasses on the yachts in the bay. Ingrid and Chris were married, their yacht had slipped out of harbour and they had gone on their honeymoon, and she doubted whether Chris's father would still be alive when they returned. He had insisted, nevertheless, that Chris and Ingrid go: he was happy that they were married. As Aileen Selby was. For it was over – the anxiety, the worry, the despair and the horror.

The sun was hot, burning the back of her neck. But it was not as hot as the Australian sun, that sun so many years ago, the sun that had burned her while she lay with a man she had now almost forgotten. It had been an infatuation, a wild desire compounded of excitement and puberty and rebellion. Her father would not see reason, she had wanted to marry, so she had allowed Schulman to take her, they had loved, and she had felt life move inside her. That had been a proud moment, the first time the child moved.

Her father had hit her when she told him.

It could have been good, she thought that even now, it could have been good and peaceful, but Kurt Schulman was German and her father hated him. She had thought the child, when it came, would heal the wounds, create something for Kurt and herself.

The child came, and her world exploded.

She focused the field glasses again and saw the launch driving a white furrow across the blue water, headed for the bay and the hill. It bore a small flag on the stern: an official police boat. She had seen others, in the harbour. She put down the glasses and shielded her face against the sun, trying to sleep.

Sleep would not come. It had eluded her, other than fitfully, for weeks, and it eluded her now. For the horror would not be dispelled. Whichever way one looked ugliness came. It had been with her from that day when Erich was born, in 1946. It had faded, she had pushed the word to the back of her mind and watched Ingrid grow, mature into a beautiful woman, but then it had come back to her in its full horror that day when the phone rang.

'It's Erich,' the man had said. 'You *must*

remember me. Can a woman forget her son?'

His voice had been laughing, bantering, but it was different when she picked him up in the Volvo and at his direction drove out to Lockyer's Tarn. She had sat beside him, her son, but he was a stranger, a vicious, embittered stranger who mocked her, railed at her for deserting him as a child, for staining his blood with disease, for ruining his life. She wanted to explain about his father, how she had not been able to face the pressures of the time, her father's disapproval, Kurt's background, a haemophiliac child, but she couldn't because she began to realize Erich Schulman's intention.

'Look around you,' he had said, 'look around at this dark gloomy lake, at the crags, the silence and the loneliness and see, see my life. This is why we meet here, *Mother,* so that you can understand.'

Mother. But he could not be her son, not this evil, violent man, with his threats.

'For it's time you paid,' he had said. 'For all the years I was alone and in fear of this sickness. I saw your photograph in a French magazine – mother of the bride – and I knew it was time you paid. And it will be much – to make up for the years and the dread.'

Ingrid. The child, the daughter she had

cherished even though she had never wanted to conceive her for she had feared a second conception – the daughter whom she had worked for, the daughter who had met Chris Santer, was about to contract a brilliant marriage, it was Ingrid whom Erich threatened to destroy. For if he had no happiness, neither should she, for she could be a *carrier*. Would Santer marry her then? Would the old man allow his son to marry Ingrid Selby and perhaps have a haemophiliac grandson?

It was then that Aileen Selby had murdered her son. It had been quick and effortless. She had leaned forward, opened the glove compartment, turned with the gun in her hand and shot him as he sat. He had made no sign and no sound. He had died almost instantly. She had felt no emotion.

And now she tried to forget the deliberateness with which she had placed that gun in the car before driving out that night; tried to forget the way she had heaved and tugged the body into the back, driven the car to the crag, released the brake and allowed it to drop into the tarn, trudged back to the house, unfeeling, unthinking, *dead*. She had killed her son, but he had been no son, a stranger, the guilt of a past she regretted, a present she feared.

But Ingrid, she thought, was safe.

Then the second call came.

The heartbeats were stilling, the panic had died, she had begun to relax and forget the horror, and she was with Ingrid, preparing for the wedding, when the second man rang.

'My name is Rutland,' he said. 'I knew Erich – and *I know where he is now.*'

Dully, she had agreed to return home. She had flown back, arrived at Bradford Airport in the early hours of the morning and driven to Earston. There was nothing in her mind then, nothing but defeat. She had failed, Erich had won, Ingrid's life could still be shattered.

She could remember the oblong of light and the shadow of a man, the sound of running feet. She had waited, walked towards the bungalow and there the solution lay for her, ugly, battered, bloody, but breathing.

Soon, he had stopped breathing, and it was in utter calm that she had returned to Selby Grange. It was over, and done.

She turned over to lie on her stomach. The launch had beached and a small group of men were standing at the jetty. They seemed to be looking up towards the hill, and as she watched they began to walk towards the crude steps cut out of the rock below her. She raised her field glasses, and the faces came up in her vision, blurs of faces, sharp under the peaked caps, but featureless at this distance. Except one: no uniform, no cap, but a white skull that shone in the sunlight.

Aileen Selby rose to her feet, slowly. Ingrid and Chris were gone. There was only the guilt and the horror hanging over her like a vulture, waiting for the end. She remembered the pain of her youth, the agony of the truth for a twenty-year-old girl, the weakness and fear that made her turn her back on her son, the hatred that made her kill him, finally. And she remembered the feel of a poker head, hammering into the splintered skull of a dying blackmailer.

She could face it no longer, she could think of it no more. The horror in her own blood was not necessarily in Ingrid's; Ingrid might never know.

Chief Inspector Crow was an ugly man, but she had detected compassion in him. It was the last thought, and hope, in her mind when she missed the step hewn at the top of the crag and fluttered downwards to the silence.

John Crow didn't know whether Wilson

would agree, but he didn't give a damn. There was nothing to be gained by exposure. The local police knew he wanted to interview Mrs Selby and little more; now she was dead. Chris Santer and Ingrid had their own lives to lead, their own problems to solve, their own crises to surmount.

He agreed with the local chief of police that a telephone call should be made immediately, to acquaint Ingrid Santer of the accidental death of her mother. He agreed that Chris Santer's father should not be informed at once, in view of his heart condition – it should be left to his son to impart the news. He gave no details of the reasons for his request to interview Mrs Selby.

Eight hours later he flew home.

He filed his reports at Scotland Yard, bought a paper to read on the way home and learned that Conrad Gunther had returned to South America. There were rumours in Fleet Street about certain Nazi connections.

Martha was waiting when Crow got home. He felt little like celebrating, but he took her out to dinner in a quiet restaurant. She ordered duck a l'orange.

So did he.

253

The publishers hope that this book has given you enjoyable reading. Large Print Books are especially designed to be as easy to see and hold as possible. If you wish a complete list of our books please ask at your local library or write directly to:

Magna Large Print Books
Magna House, Long Preston,
Skipton, North Yorkshire.
BD23 4ND

This Large Print Book, for people
who cannot read normal print,
is published under the auspices of

THE ULVERSCROFT FOUNDATION